the Smurfs™

CHRISTMAS

A **SMURFS** GRAPHIC NOVEL BY *Peyo*

PAPERCUTZ™

NEW YORK

SMURFS GRAPHIC NOVELS AVAILABLE FROM PAPERCUTZ™

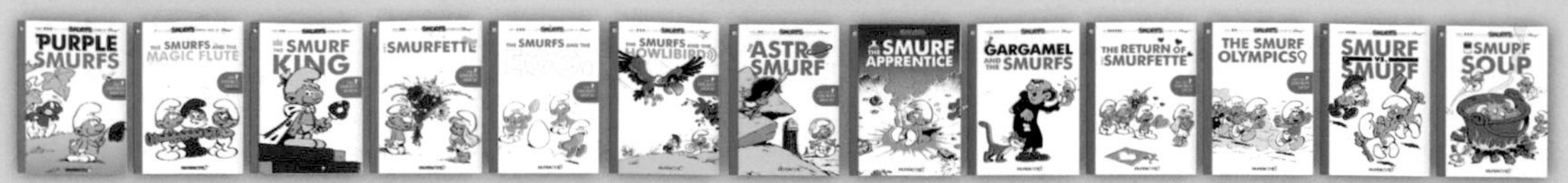

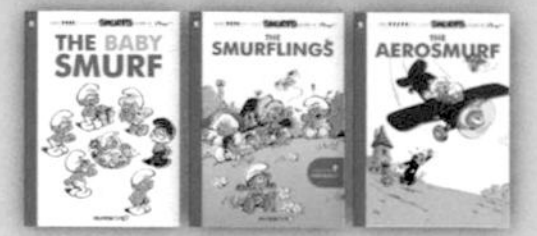

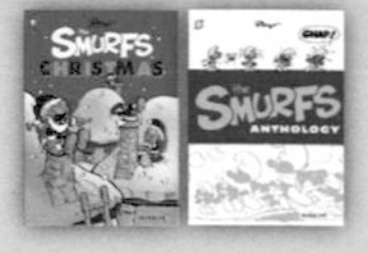

1. THE PURPLE SMURFS
2. THE SMURFS AND THE MAGIC FLUTE
3. THE SMURF KING
4. THE SMURFETTE
5. THE SMURFS AND THE EGG
6. THE SMURFS AND THE HOWLIBIRD
7. THE ASTROSMURF
8. THE SMURF APPRENTICE
9. GARGAMEL AND THE SMURFS
10. THE RETURN OF THE SMURFETTE
11. THE SMURF OLYMPICS
12. SMURF VS. SMURF
13. SMURF SOUP
14. THE BABY SMURF
15. THE SMURFLINGS
16. THE AEROSMURF

THE SMURFS CHRISTMAS
THE SMURFS ANTHOLOGY VOL. 1

COMING SOON:

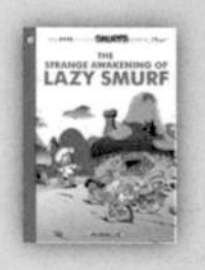

17. THE STRANGE AWAKENING OF LAZY SMURF

THE SMURFS graphic novels, including THE SMURFS CHRISTMAS, are available in paperback for $5.99 each and in hardcover for $10.99 each at booksellers everywhere. THE SMURFS ANTHOLOGY is available only in hardcover for $19.99 each.You can also order online at www.papercutz.com. Or call 1-800-886-1223, Monday through Friday, 9 – 5 EST. MC, Visa, and AmEx accepted. To order by mail, please add $4.00 for postage and handling for first book ordered, $1.00 for each additional book and make check payable to NBM Publishing. Send to: Papercutz, 160 Broadway, Suite 700, East Wing, New York, NY 10038.

THE SMURFS graphic novels are also available digitally wherever e-books are sold.

WWW.PAPERCUTZ.COM

THE SMURFS CHRISTMAS

"Little Peter's Christmas"
BY PEYO

"The Ogre and the Smurfs"
BY PEYO

"Strange Snowmen"
BY PEYO

"Hibernatus Smurfimus"
BY PEYO

"The Little Tree"
BY PEYO

"The Smurfs Christmas"
BY PEYO

Joe Johnson, *SMURFLATIONS*
Adam Grano, *SMURFIC DESIGN*
Janice Chiang, *LETTERING SMURFETTE*
Matt. Murray, *SMURF CONSULTANT*
Beth Scorzato, *SMURF COORDINATOR*
Michael Petranek, *ASSOCIATE SMURF*
Jim Salicrup, *SMURF-IN-CHIEF*

PAPERBACK EDITION ISBN: 978-1-59707-451-3
HARDCOVER EDITION ISBN: 978-1-59707-452-0

PRINTED IN CHINA SEPTEMBER 2013 BY WKT CO. LTD.
3/F PHASE I LEADER INDUSTRIAL CENTRE
188 TEXACO ROAD, TSEUN WAN, N.T., HONG KONG

Papercutz books may be purchased for business or promotional use. For information on bulk purchases please contact Macmillan Corporate and Premium Sales Department at (800) 221-7945 x5442.

DISTRIBUTED BY MACMILLAN
FIRST PAPERCUTZ PRINTING

LITTLE PETER'S CHRISTMAS

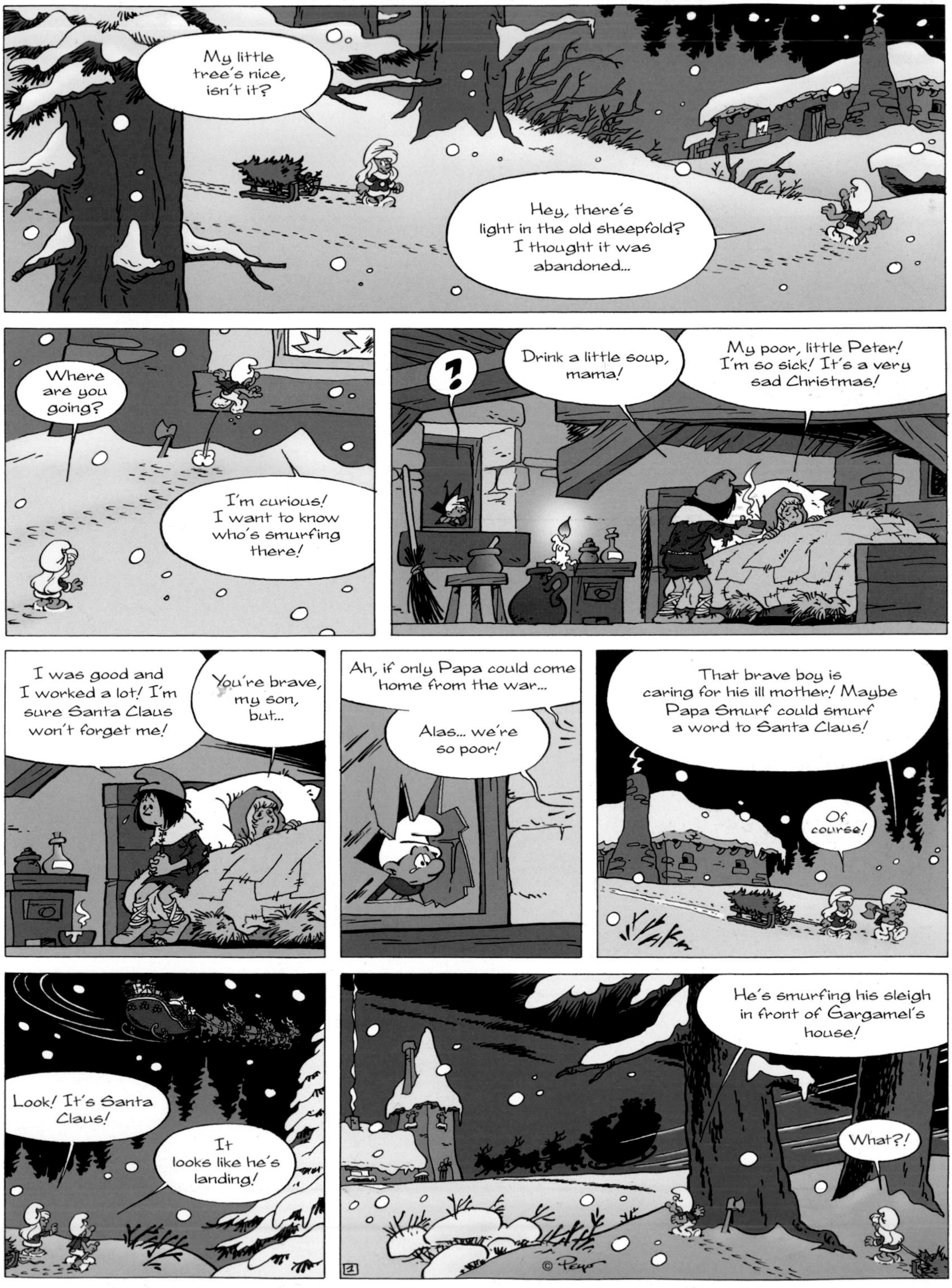
My little tree's nice, isn't it?
Hey, there's light in the old sheepfold? I thought it was abandoned...
Where are you going?
I'm curious! I want to know who's smurfing there!
?
Drink a little soup, mama!
My poor, little Peter! I'm so sick! It's a very sad Christmas!
I was good and I worked a lot! I'm sure Santa Claus won't forget me!
You're brave, my son, but...
Ah, if only Papa could come home from the war...
Alas... we're so poor!
That brave boy is caring for his ill mother! Maybe Papa Smurf could smurf a word to Santa Claus!
Of course!
Look! It's Santa Claus!
It looks like he's landing!
He's smurfing his sleigh in front of Gargamel's house!
What?!
1
© Peyo

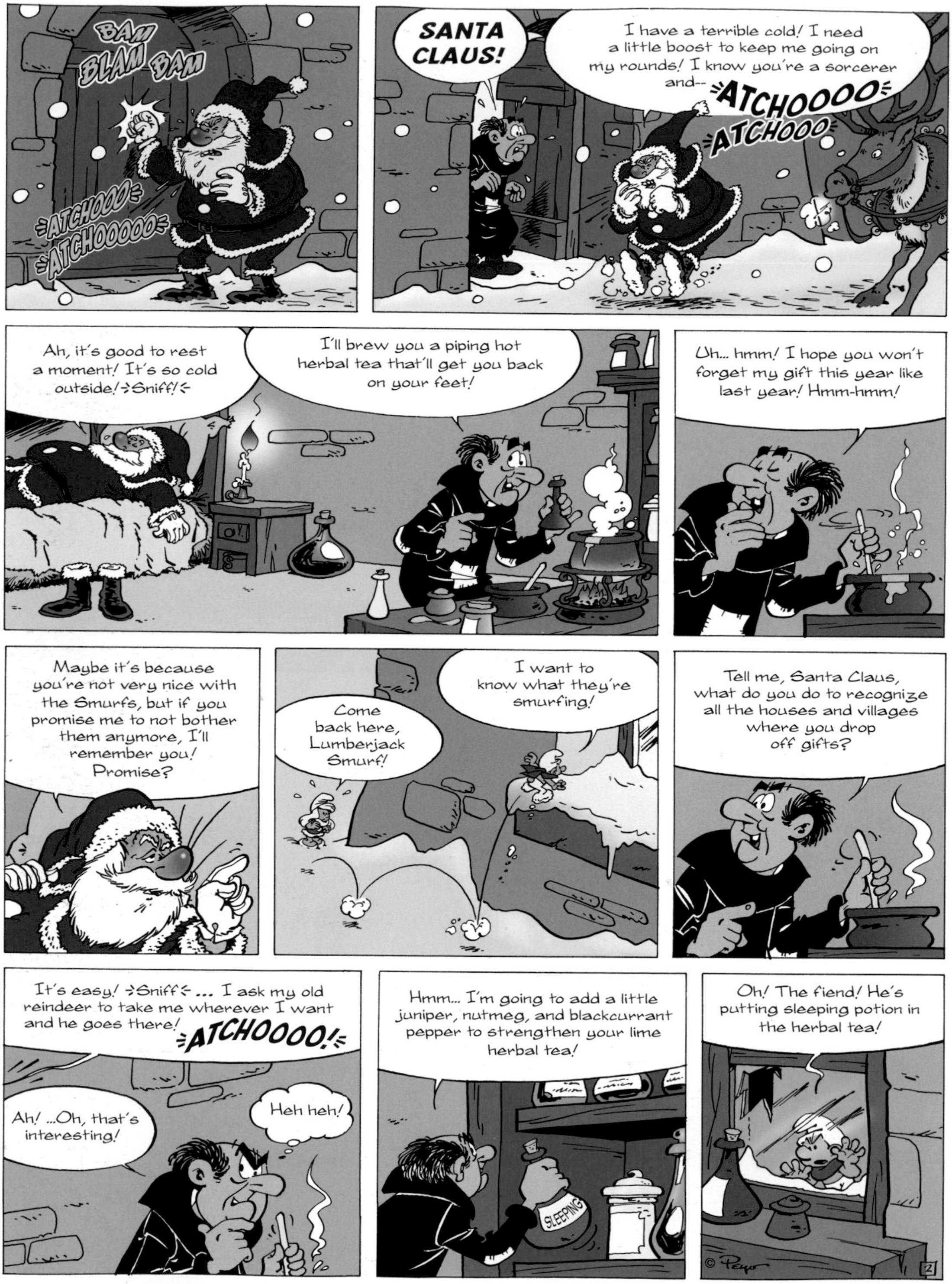
BAM
BLAM BAM
ATCHOOO
ATCHOOOOO
SANTA CLAUS!
I have a terrible cold! I need a little boost to keep me going on my rounds! I know you're a sorcerer and--
ATCHOOOO
ATCHOOO
Ah, it's good to rest a moment! It's so cold outside! Sniff!
I'll brew you a piping hot herbal tea that'll get you back on your feet!
Uh... hmm! I hope you won't forget my gift this year like last year! Hmm-hmm!
Maybe it's because you're not very nice with the Smurfs, but if you promise me to not bother them anymore, I'll remember you! Promise?
Come back here, Lumberjack Smurf!
I want to know what they're smurfing!
Tell me, Santa Claus, what do you do to recognize all the houses and villages where you drop off gifts?
It's easy! Sniff ... I ask my old reindeer to take me wherever I want and he goes there!
ATCHOOOO!
Ah! ...Oh, that's interesting!
Heh heh!
Hmm... I'm going to add a little juniper, nutmeg, and blackcurrant pepper to strengthen your lime herbal tea!
SLEEPING
Oh! The fiend! He's putting sleeping potion in the herbal tea!
© Peyo
2

⇒Slurp⇐ ... hmm! It's hot! It's good!

Have another little cup then!

⇒AAAAAH!⇐ That's better! I already feel like a new man... I'm sleepy...

It wasn't easy getting his clothes off, but I did it! It's up to me to take advantage of this! Heh heh heh!

He smurfed on a fake beard to disguise himself as Santa Claus!

!

Let's go! Those cursed Smurfs will get a nasty surprise for their Christmas gift! Heh heh!

OH!

Are you the old reindeer? I want you to take me to the Smurf Village right away, understood?

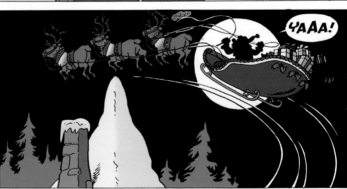

YAAA!

What do we do? We'll never smurf there in time to warn Papa Smurf!

Our only hope is to smurf Santa Claus from his sleep! Come on!

© Peyo

SANTA CLAUS! WAKE UP! THE SMURFS ARE IN DANGER!

⇒RZZ⇐

It's no use! I'm smurfing his beard, but it's having no effect on him!

I found a potion that'll smurf him!

⇒RZ⇐

3

7

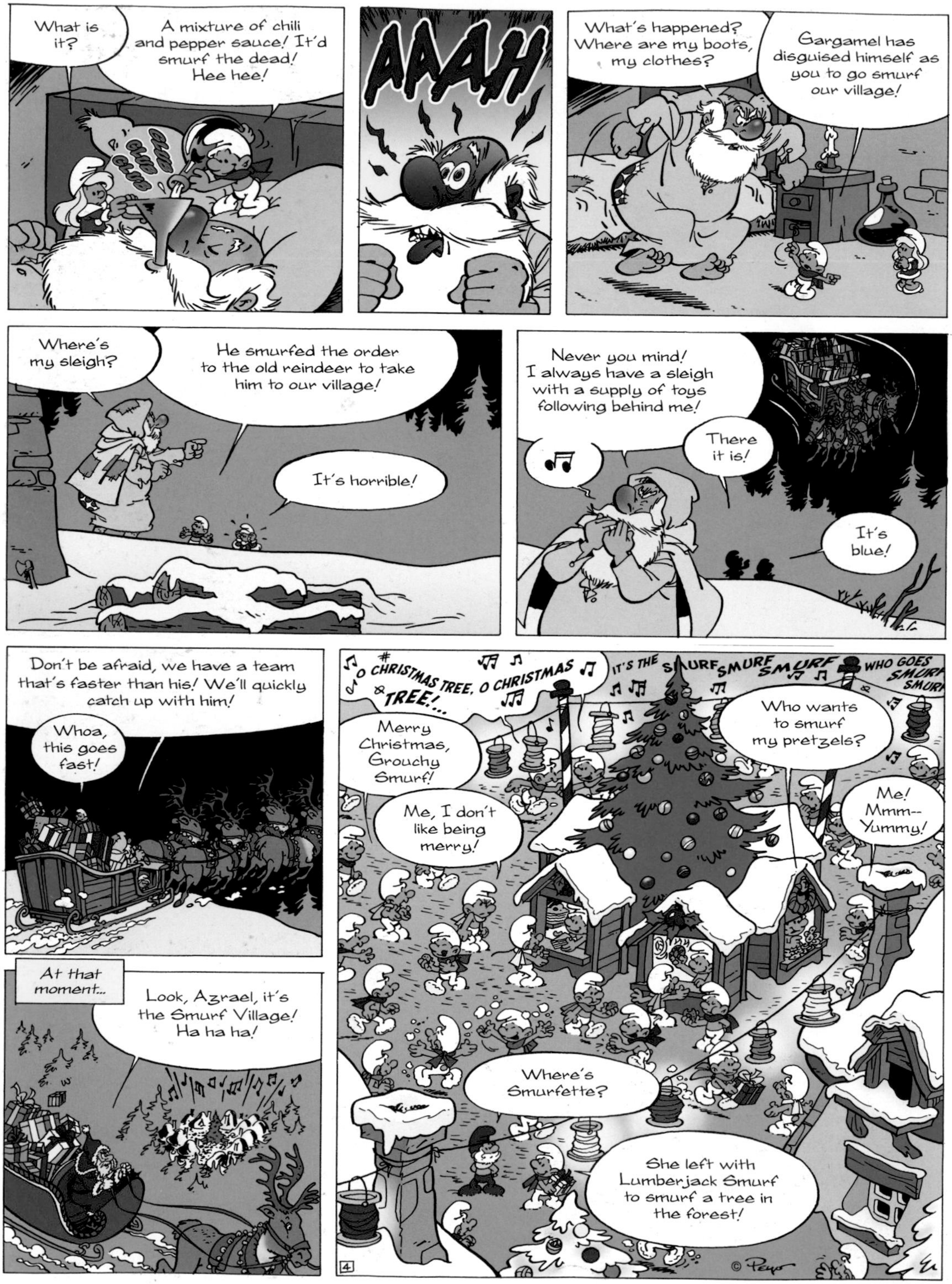
What is it?
A mixture of chili and pepper sauce! It'd smurf the dead! Hee hee!
GLUB GLUB GLUB
AAAH
What's happened? Where are my boots, my clothes?
Gargamel has disguised himself as you to go smurf our village!
Where's my sleigh?
He smurfed the order to the old reindeer to take him to our village!
It's horrible!
Never you mind! I always have a sleigh with a supply of toys following behind me!
There it is!
It's blue!
Don't be afraid, we have a team that's faster than his! We'll quickly catch up with him!
Whoa, this goes fast!
At that moment...
Look, Azrael, it's the Smurf Village! Ha ha ha!
O CHRISTMAS TREE, O CHRISTMAS TREE!...
IT'S THE SMURF SMURF SMURF WHO GOES
Merry Christmas, Grouchy Smurf!
Me, I don't like being merry!
Who wants to smurf my pretzels?
Me! Mmm-- Yummy!
Where's Smurfette?
She left with Lumberjack Smurf to smurf a tree in the forest!
4
© Peyo

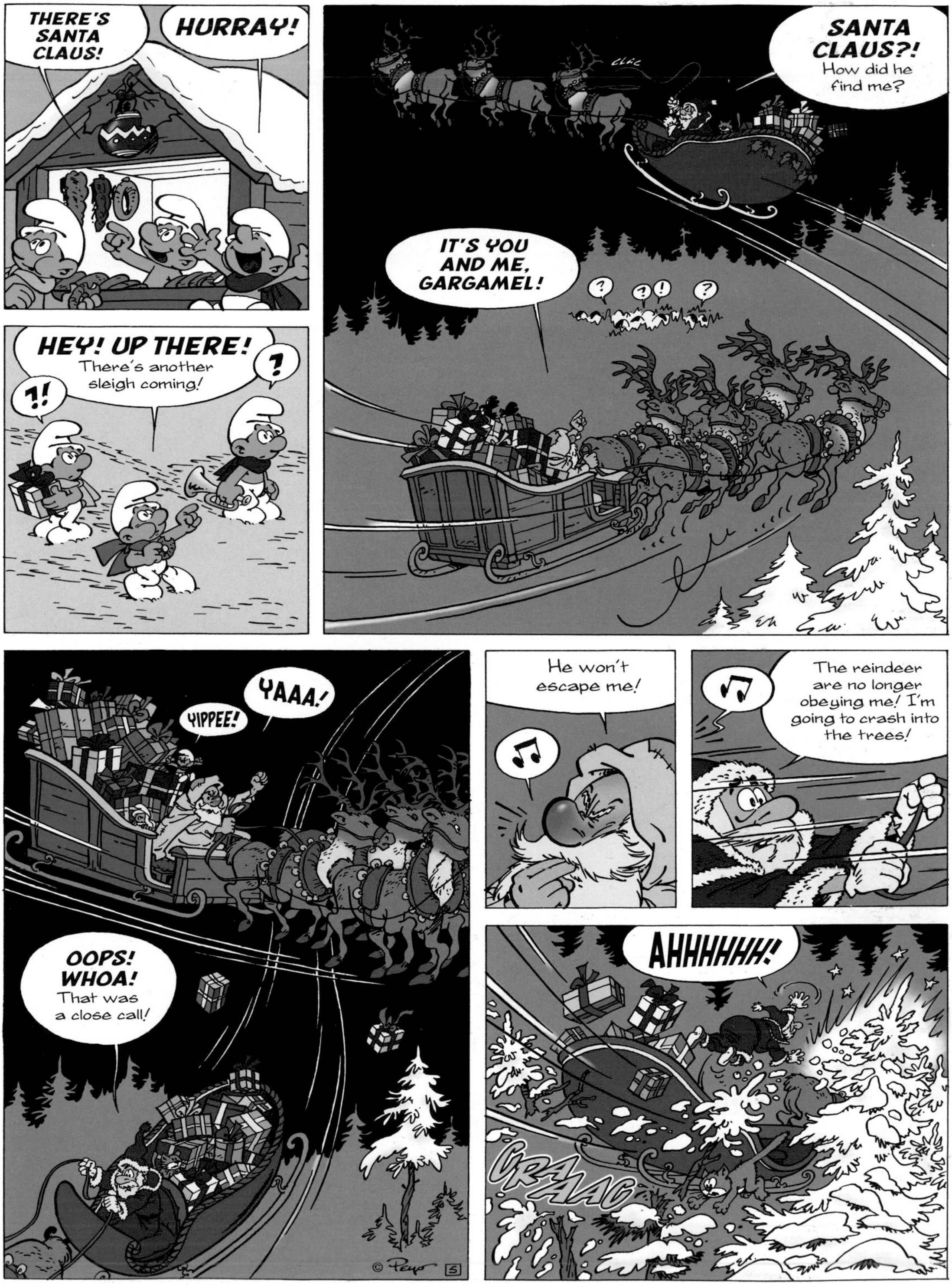
THERE'S SANTA CLAUS!
HURRAY!
SANTA CLAUS?! How did he find me?
IT'S YOU AND ME, GARGAMEL!
HEY! UP THERE! There's another sleigh coming!
?!
?
YIPPEE!
YAAA!
OOPS! WHOA! That was a close call!
He won't escape me!
The reindeer are no longer obeying me! I'm going to crash into the trees!
AHHHHHH!
CRAAAC
© Peyo

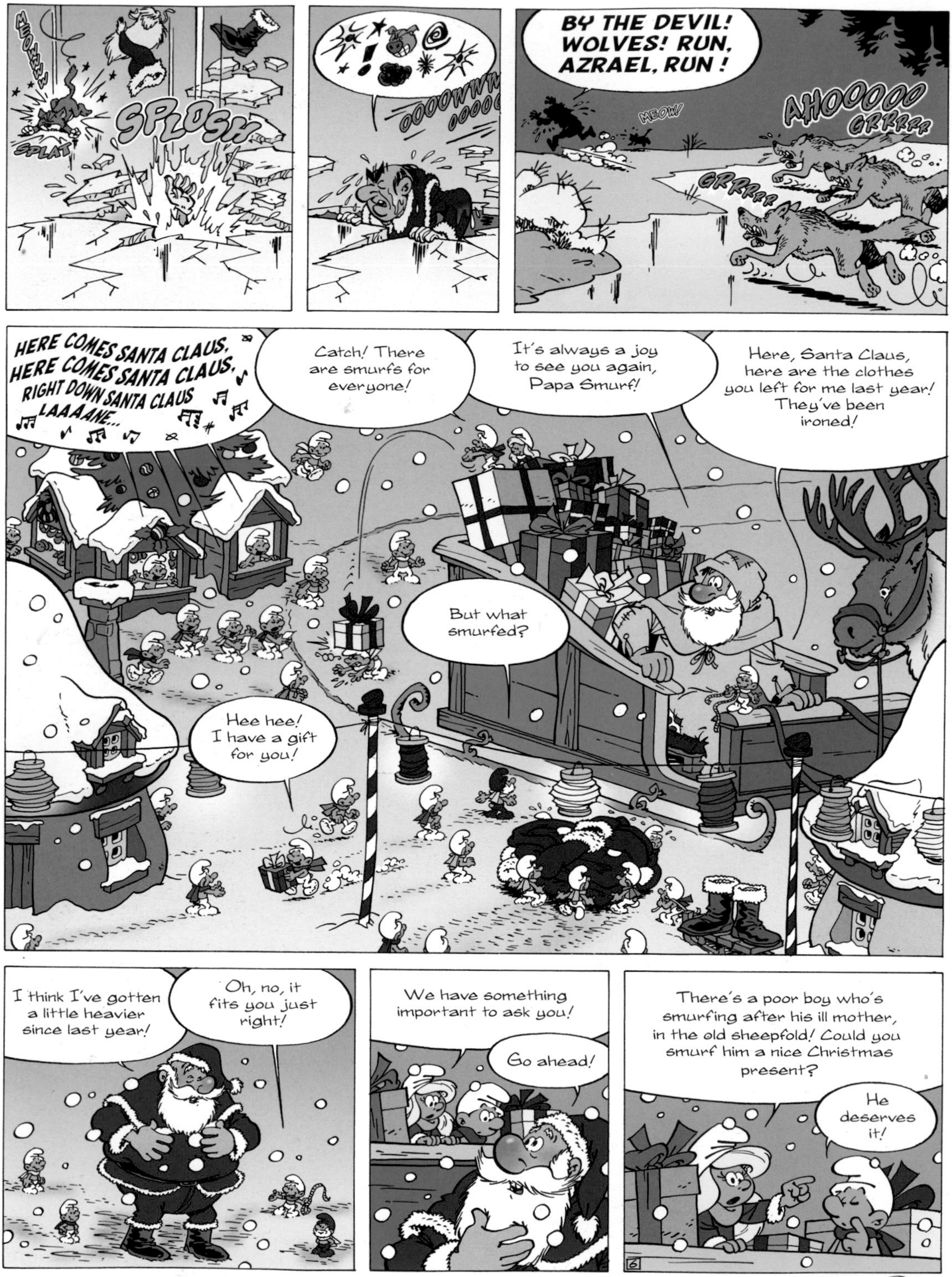
MEOWWW
SPLAT
SPLOSH
OOOOWWWW OOOOO
BY THE DEVIL! WOLVES! RUN, AZRAEL, RUN!
MEOW!
AHOOOOO GRRRRR
GRRRRR
HERE COMES SANTA CLAUS, HERE COMES SANTA CLAUS, RIGHT DOWN SANTA CLAUS LAAAANE...
Catch! There are smurfs for everyone!
It's always a joy to see you again, Papa Smurf!
Here, Santa Claus, here are the clothes you left for me last year! They've been ironed!
But what smurfed?
Hee hee! I have a gift for you!
I think I've gotten a little heavier since last year!
Oh, no, it fits you just right!
We have something important to ask you!
Go ahead!
There's a poor boy who's smurfing after his ill mother, in the old sheepfold! Could you smurf him a nice Christmas present?
He deserves it!
6

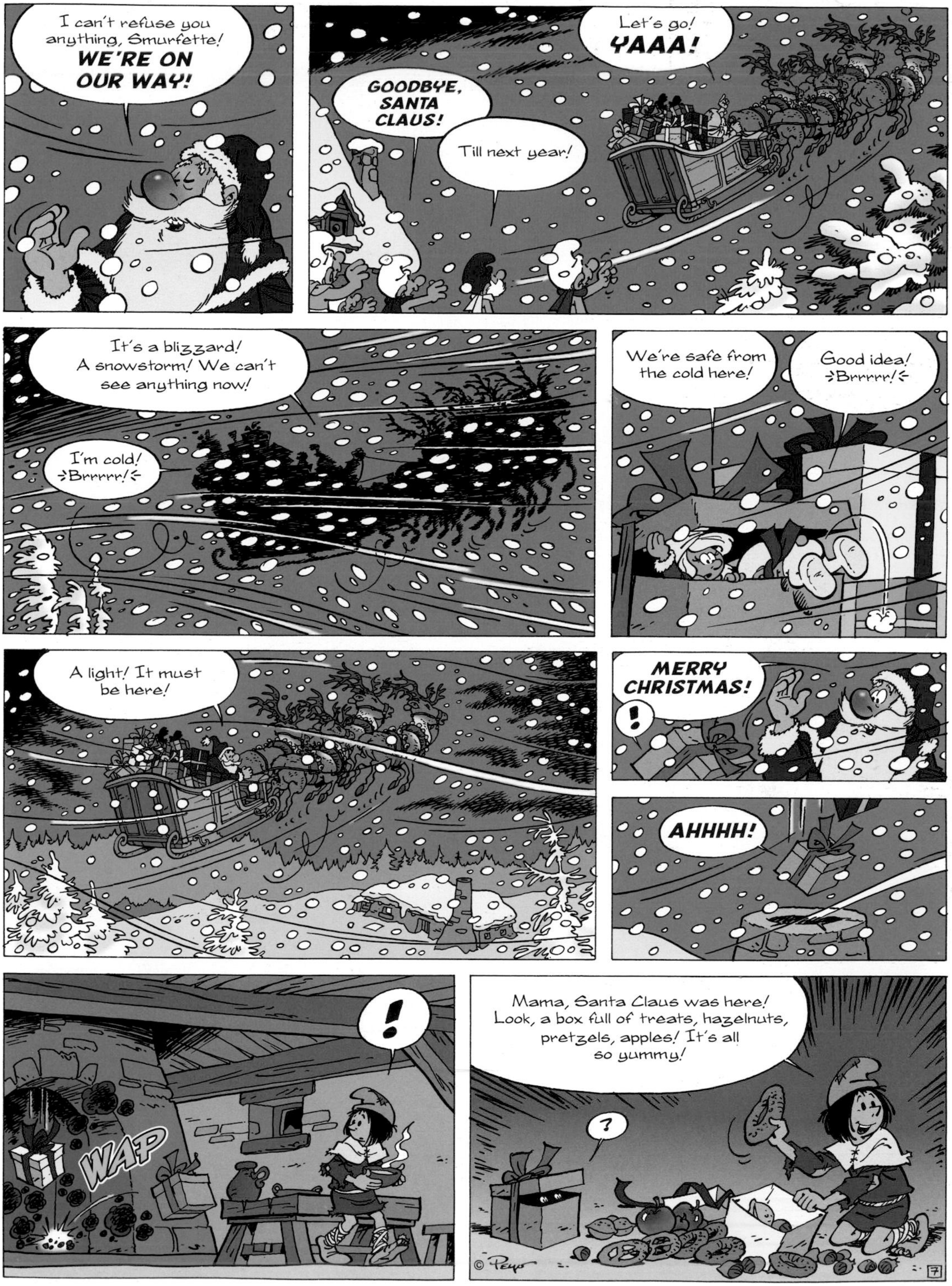

I can't refuse you anything, Smurfette! WE'RE ON OUR WAY!
GOODBYE, SANTA CLAUS!
Till next year!
Let's go! YAAA!
It's a blizzard! A snowstorm! We can't see anything now!
I'm cold! Brrrrr!
We're safe from the cold here!
Good idea! Brrrrr!
A light! It must be here!
MERRY CHRISTMAS!
!
AHHHH!
!
WAP
Mama, Santa Claus was here! Look, a box full of treats, hazelnuts, pretzels, apples! It's all so yummy!
?
© Peyo
7

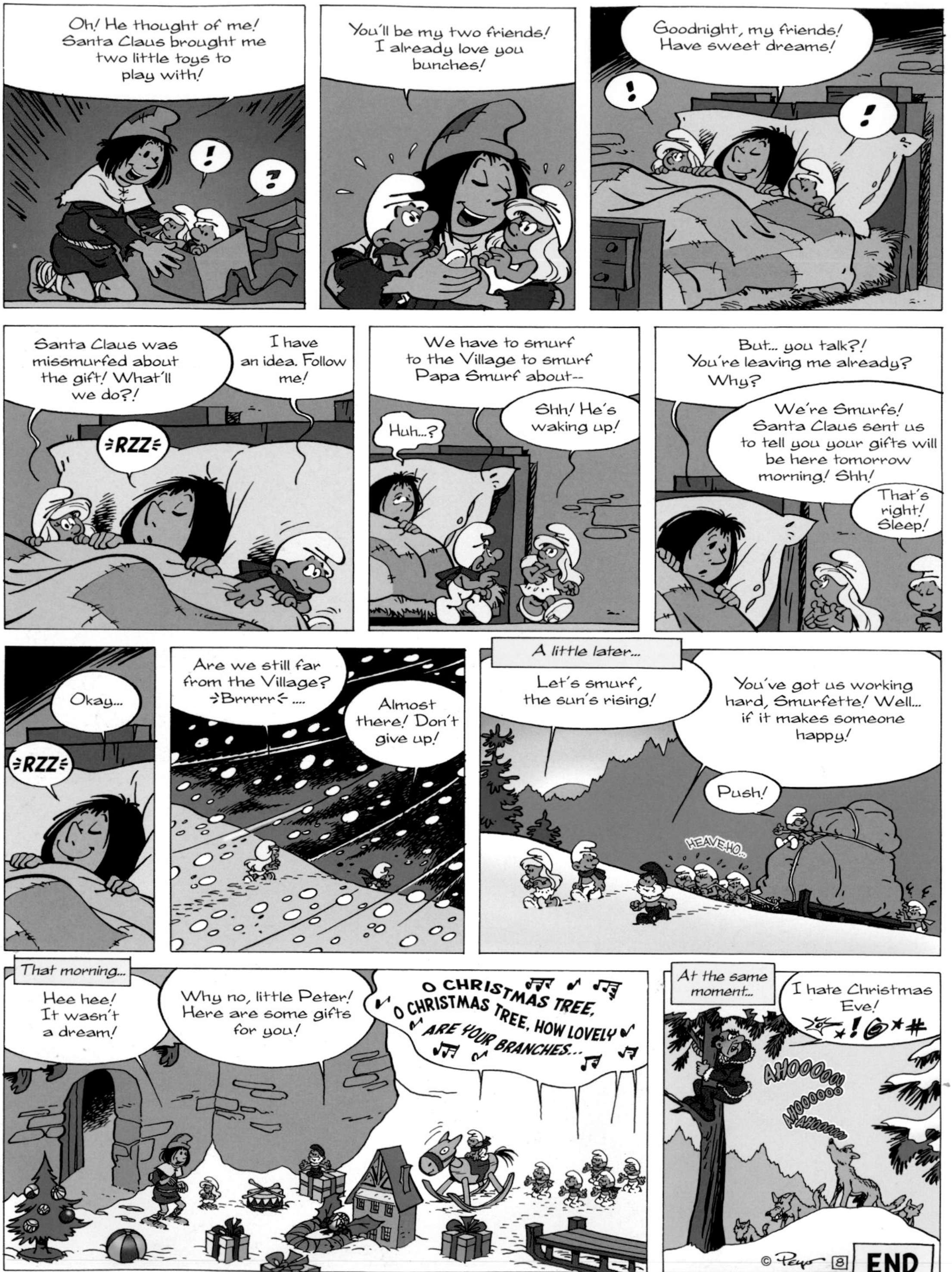

Oh! He thought of me! Santa Claus brought me two little toys to play with!
!
?
You'll be my two friends! I already love you bunches!
Goodnight, my friends! Have sweet dreams!
!
!
Santa Claus was missmurfed about the gift! What'll we do?!
I have an idea. Follow me!
RZZ
We have to smurf to the Village to smurf Papa Smurf about--
Huh...?
Shh! He's waking up!
But... you talk?! You're leaving me already? Why?
We're Smurfs! Santa Claus sent us to tell you your gifts will be here tomorrow morning! Shh!
That's right! Sleep!
Okay...
RZZ
Are we still far from the Village? Brrrrr ....
Almost there! Don't give up!
A little later...
Let's smurf, the sun's rising!
You've got us working hard, Smurfette! Well... if it makes someone happy!
Push!
HEAVE-HO...
That morning...
Hee hee! It wasn't a dream!
Why no, little Peter! Here are some gifts for you!
O CHRISTMAS TREE, O CHRISTMAS TREE, HOW LOVELY ARE YOUR BRANCHES...
At the same moment...
I hate Christmas Eve!
AHOOOOOO
AHOOOOOO
AHOOOOOO
© Peyo 8
END

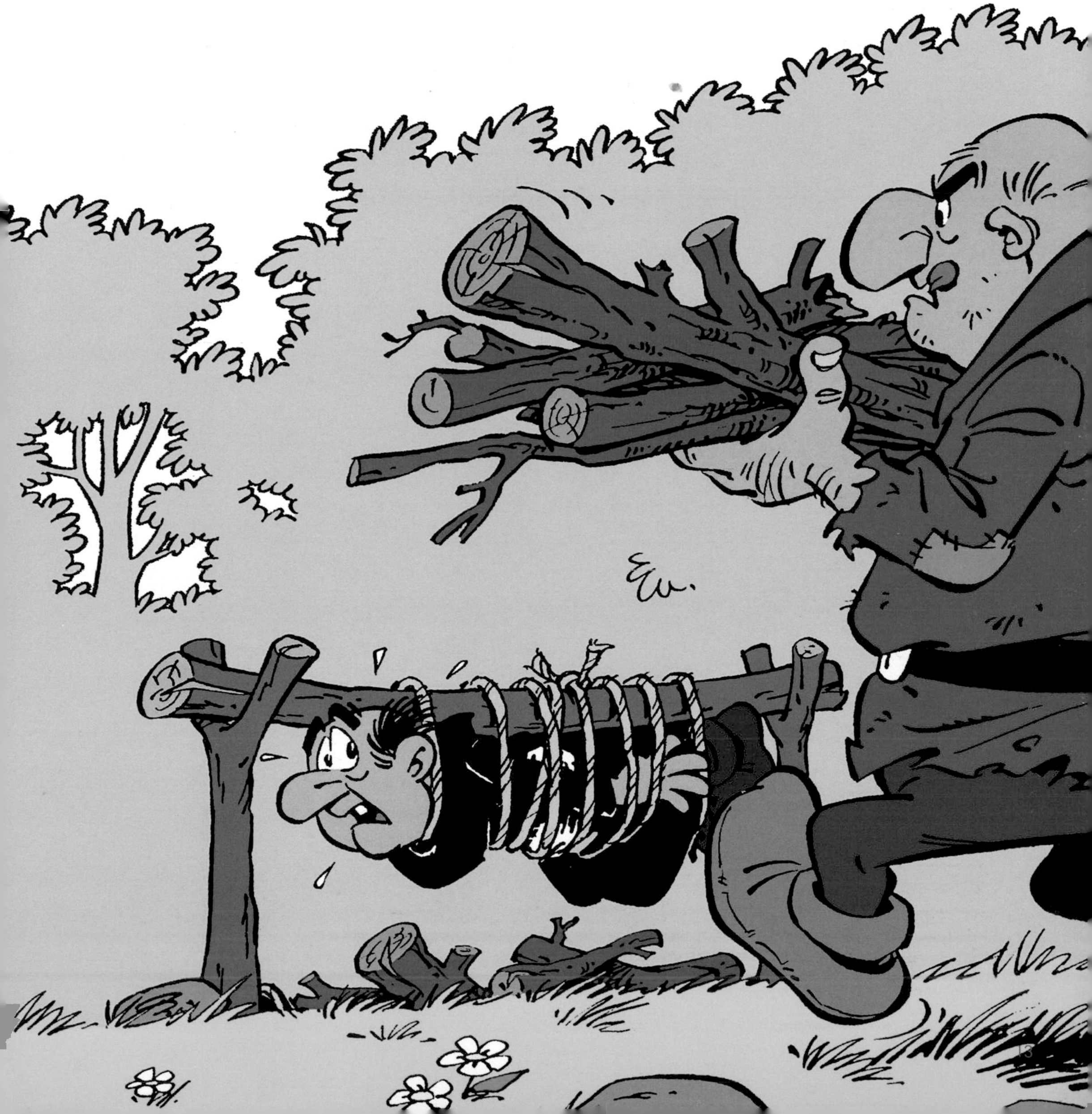

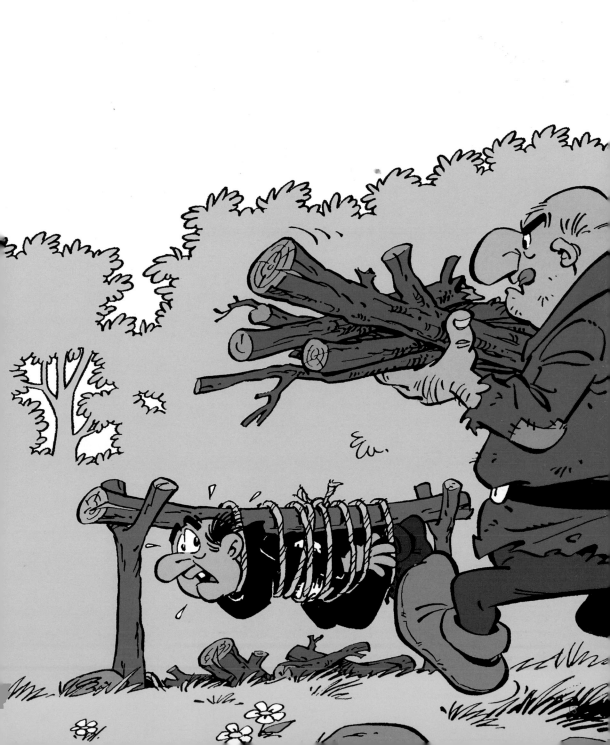

THE OGRE AND THE SMURFS

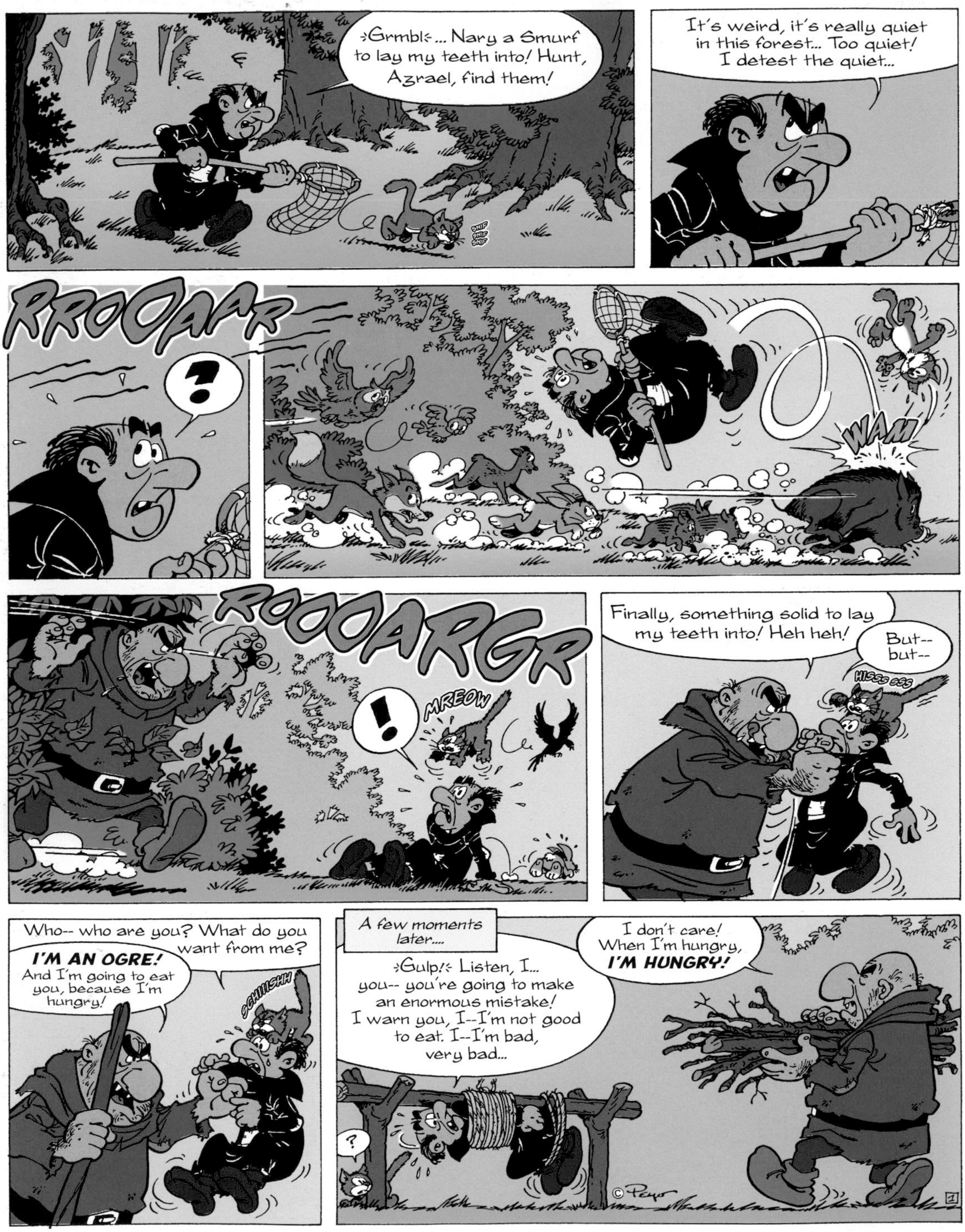

:Grmbl: ... Nary a Smurf to lay my teeth into! Hunt, Azrael, find them!
SNIF SNIF SNIF
It's weird, it's really quiet in this forest... Too quiet! I detest the quiet...
RROOAAR
?
WAM
ROOOARGR
!
MREOW
Finally, something solid to lay my teeth into! Heh heh!
But-- but--
HISSS SSS
Who-- who are you? What do you want from me?
I'M AN OGRE! And I'm going to eat you, because I'm hungry!
A few moments later....
:Gulp!: Listen, I... you-- you're going to make an enormous mistake! I warn you, I--I'm not good to eat. I--I'm bad, very bad...
I don't care! When I'm hungry, I'M HUNGRY!
?
© Peyo
1

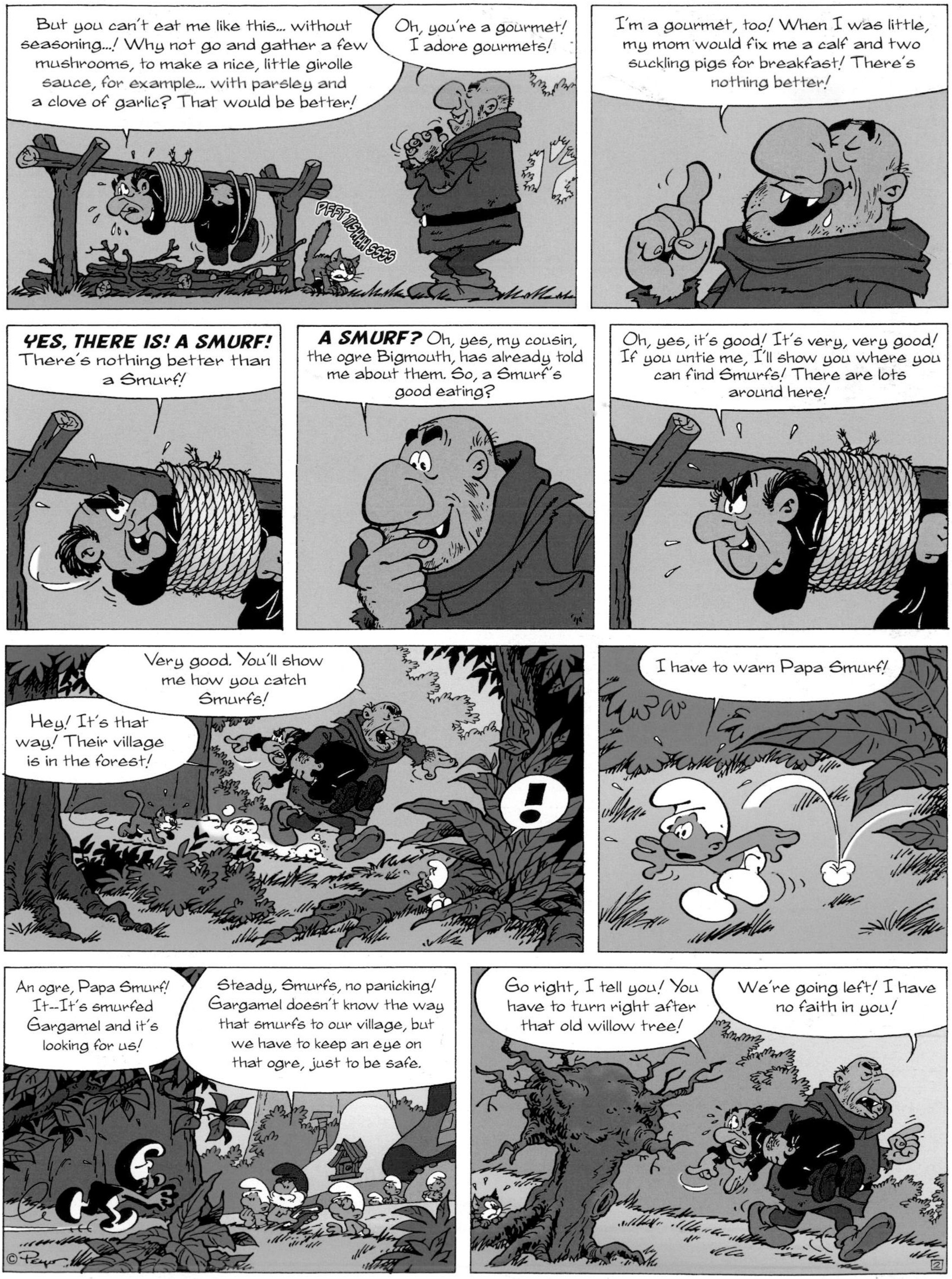
But you can't eat me like this... without seasoning...! Why not go and gather a few mushrooms, to make a nice, little girolle sauce, for example... with parsley and a clove of garlic? That would be better!
Oh, you're a gourmet! I adore gourmets!
I'm a gourmet, too! When I was little, my mom would fix me a calf and two suckling pigs for breakfast! There's nothing better!
YES, THERE IS! A SMURF! There's nothing better than a Smurf!
A SMURF? Oh, yes, my cousin, the ogre Bigmouth, has already told me about them. So, a Smurf's good eating?
Oh, yes, it's good! It's very, very good! If you untie me, I'll show you where you can find Smurfs! There are lots around here!
Very good. You'll show me how you catch Smurfs!
Hey! It's that way! Their village is in the forest!
!
I have to warn Papa Smurf!
An ogre, Papa Smurf! It--It's smurfed Gargamel and it's looking for us!
Steady, Smurfs, no panicking! Gargamel doesn't know the way that smurfs to our village, but we have to keep an eye on that ogre, just to be safe.
Go right, I tell you! You have to turn right after that old willow tree!
We're going left! I have no faith in you!
© Peyo
2

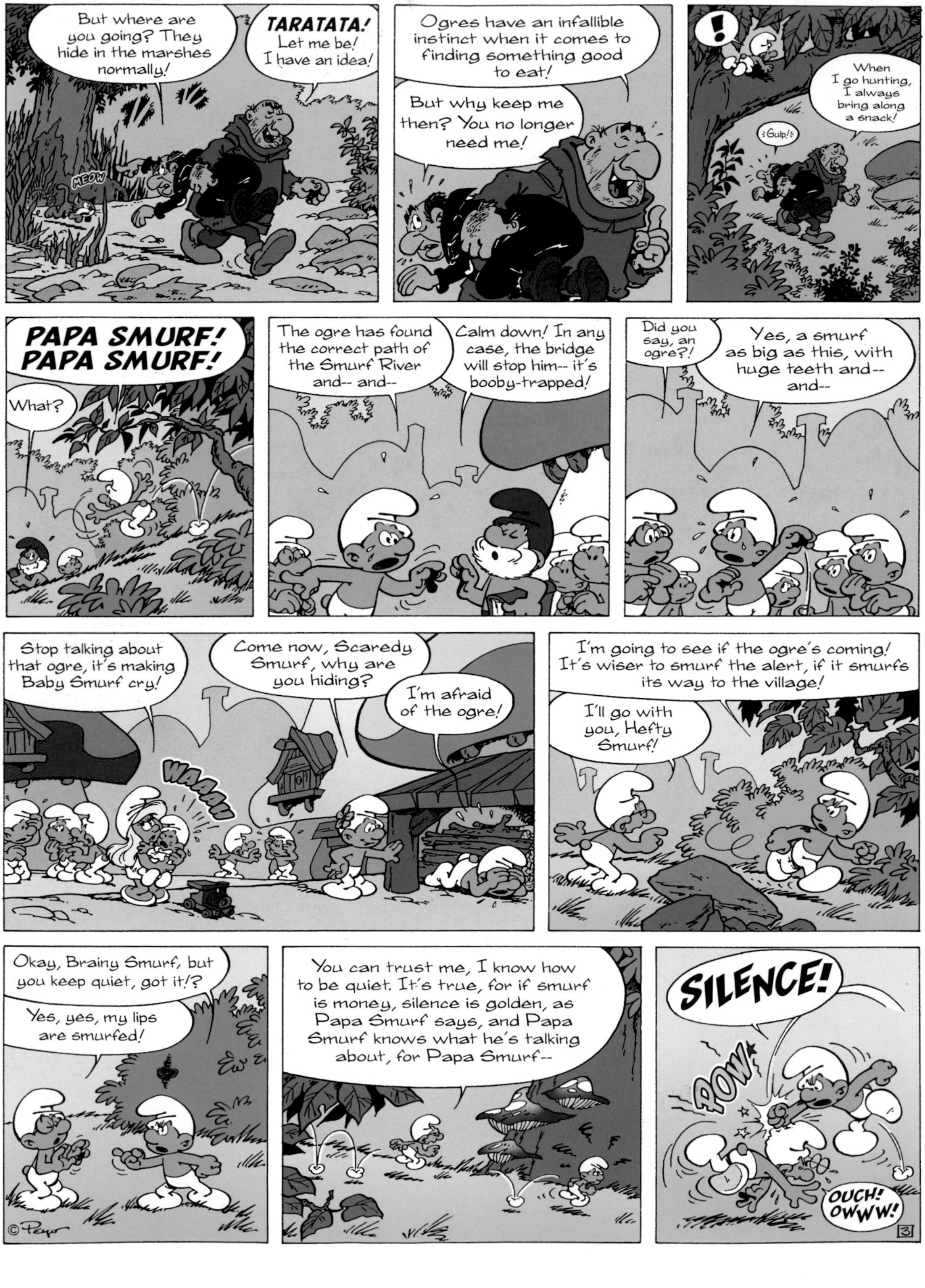

But where are you going? They hide in the marshes normally!
TARATATA! Let me be! I have an idea!
MEOW
Ogres have an infallible instinct when it comes to finding something good to eat!
But why keep me then? You no longer need me!
!
Gulp!
When I go hunting, I always bring along a snack!
PAPA SMURF! PAPA SMURF!
What?
The ogre has found the correct path of the Smurf River and-- and--
Calm down! In any case, the bridge will stop him-- it's booby-trapped!
Did you say, an ogre?!
Yes, a smurf as big as this, with huge teeth and-- and--
Stop talking about that ogre, it's making Baby Smurf cry!
Come now, Scaredy Smurf, why are you hiding?
I'm afraid of the ogre!
WAAAAH
I'm going to see if the ogre's coming! It's wiser to smurf the alert, if it smurfs its way to the village!
I'll go with you, Hefty Smurf!
Okay, Brainy Smurf, but you keep quiet, got it!?
Yes, yes, my lips are smurfed!
You can trust me, I know how to be quiet. It's true, for if smurf is money, silence is golden, as Papa Smurf says, and Papa Smurf knows what he's talking about, for Papa Smurf--
SILENCE!
POW
OUCH! OWWW!
3
© Peyo

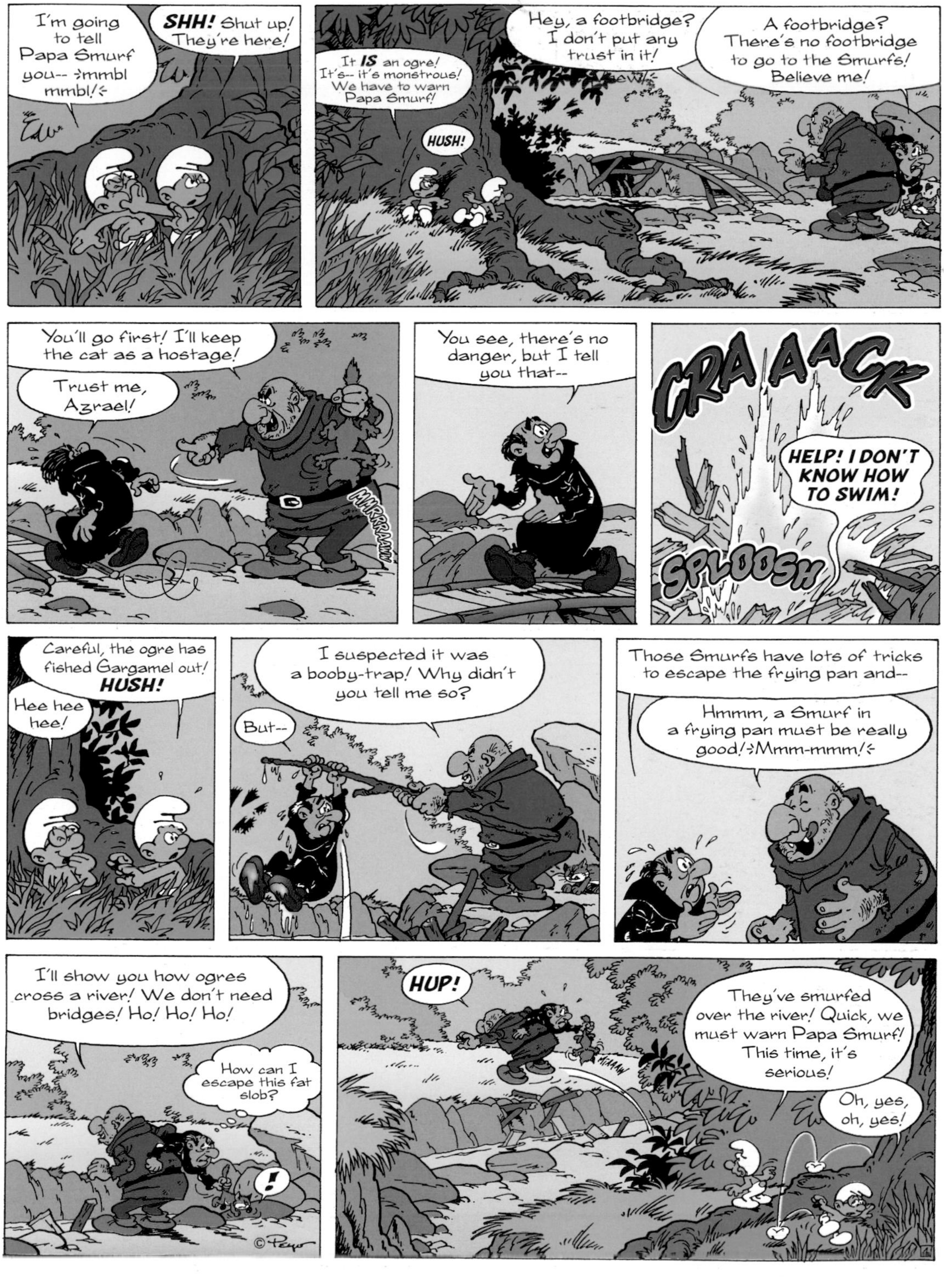
I'm going to tell Papa Smurf you-- mmbl mmbl!
SHH! Shut up! They're here!
It IS an ogre! It's-- it's monstrous! We have to warn Papa Smurf!
HUSH!
Hey, a footbridge? I don't put any trust in it!
A footbridge? There's no footbridge to go to the Smurfs! Believe me!
You'll go first! I'll keep the cat as a hostage!
Trust me, Azrael!
MARRRAAAW
You see, there's no danger, but I tell you that--
CRA AAACK
HELP! I DON'T KNOW HOW TO SWIM!
SPLOOSH
Careful, the ogre has fished Gargamel out!
HUSH!
Hee hee hee!
I suspected it was a booby-trap! Why didn't you tell me so?
But--
Those Smurfs have lots of tricks to escape the frying pan and--
Hmmm, a Smurf in a frying pan must be really good! Mmm-mmm!
I'll show you how ogres cross a river! We don't need bridges! Ho! Ho! Ho!
How can I escape this fat slob?
!
© Peyo
HUP!
They've smurfed over the river! Quick, we must warn Papa Smurf! This time, it's serious!
Oh, yes, oh, yes!

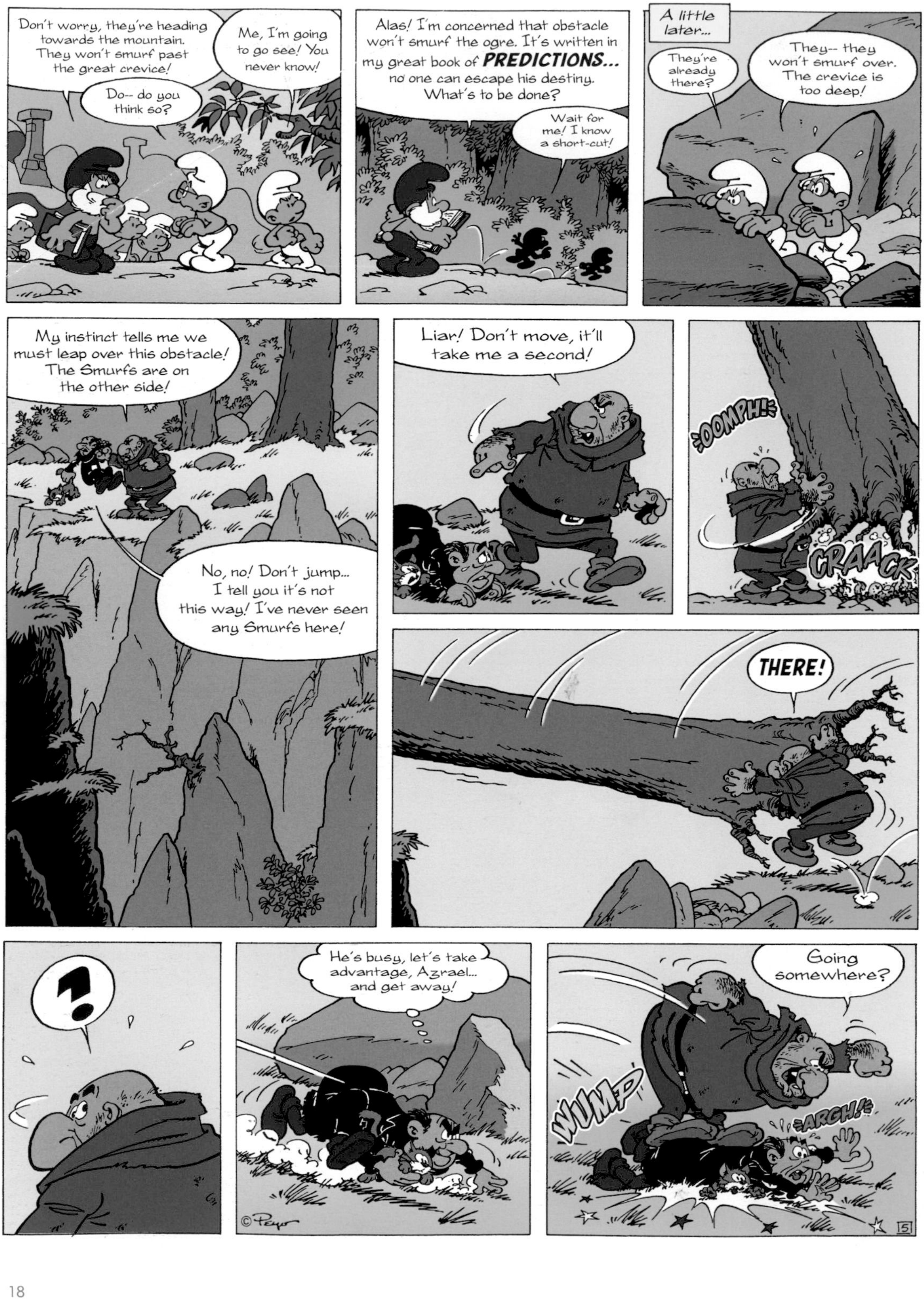
Don't worry, they're heading towards the mountain. They won't smurf past the great crevice!
Me, I'm going to go see! You never know!
Do-- do you think so?
Alas! I'm concerned that obstacle won't smurf the ogre. It's written in my great book of PREDICTIONS... no one can escape his destiny. What's to be done?
Wait for me! I know a short-cut!
A little later...
They're already there?
They-- they won't smurf over. The crevice is too deep!
My instinct tells me we must leap over this obstacle! The Smurfs are on the other side!
No, no! Don't jump... I tell you it's not this way! I've never seen any Smurfs here!
Liar! Don't move, it'll take me a second!
OOMPH!
CRAACK
THERE!
?
He's busy, let's take advantage, Azrael... and get away!
Going somewhere?
WUMP
ARGH!
© Peyo
5

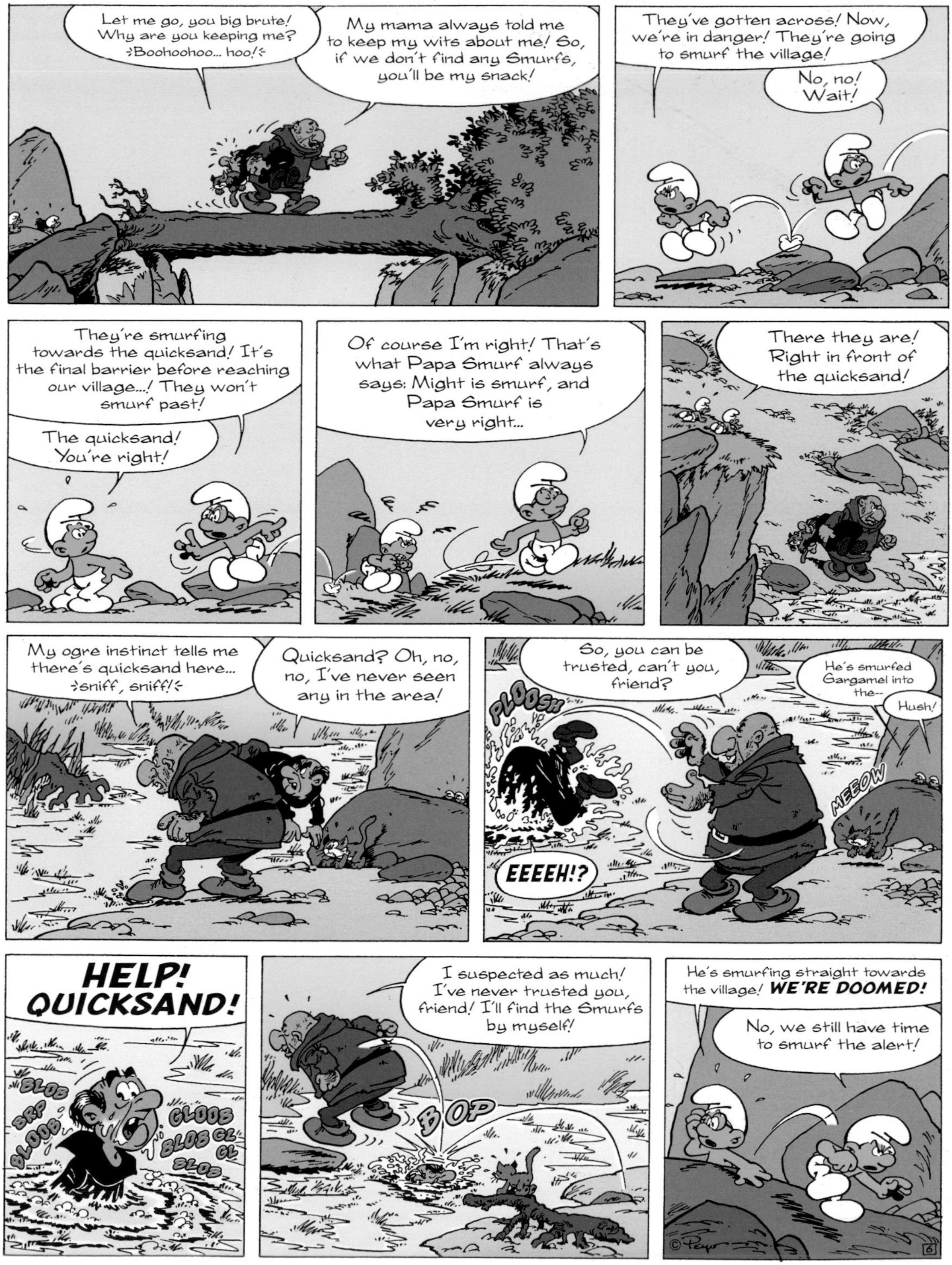
Let me go, you big brute! Why are you keeping me? ≯Boohoohoo... hoo!≮
My mama always told me to keep my wits about me! So, if we don't find any Smurfs, you'll be my snack!
They've gotten across! Now, we're in danger! They're going to smurf the village!
No, no! Wait!
They're smurfing towards the quicksand! It's the final barrier before reaching our village...! They won't smurf past!
The quicksand! You're right!
Of course I'm right! That's what Papa Smurf always says: Might is smurf, and Papa Smurf is very right...
There they are! Right in front of the quicksand!
My ogre instinct tells me there's quicksand here... ≯sniff, sniff!≮
Quicksand? Oh, no, no, I've never seen any in the area!
So, you can be trusted, can't you, friend?
PLOOSH
He's smurfed Gargamel into the--
Hush!
MEEOW
EEEEH!?
HELP! QUICKSAND!
BLOB
BRP
BLOOB
GLOOB
BLOB GL
GL
BLOB
I suspected as much! I've never trusted you, friend! I'll find the Smurfs by myself!
BOP
He's smurfing straight towards the village! **WE'RE DOOMED!**
No, we still have time to smurf the alert!
© Peyo
6

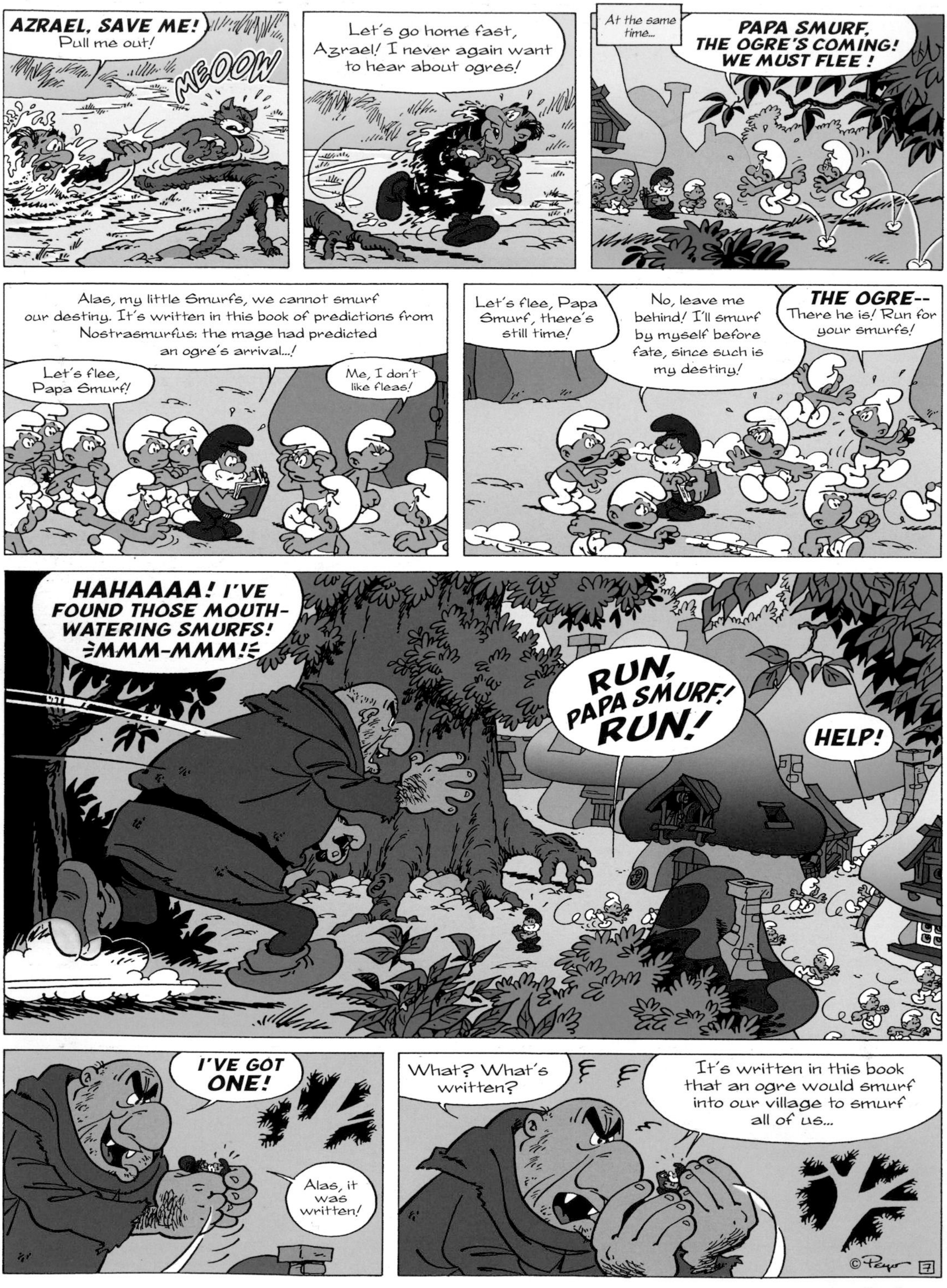
AZRAEL, SAVE ME! Pull me out!
MEOOW
Let's go home fast, Azrael! I never again want to hear about ogres!
At the same time...
PAPA SMURF, THE OGRE'S COMING! WE MUST FLEE !
Alas, my little Smurfs, we cannot smurf our destiny. It's written in this book of predictions from Nostrasmurfus: the mage had predicted an ogre's arrival...!
Let's flee, Papa Smurf!
Me, I don't like fleas!
Let's flee, Papa Smurf, there's still time!
No, leave me behind! I'll smurf by myself before fate, since such is my destiny!
THE OGRE-- There he is! Run for your smurfs!
HAHAAAA! I'VE FOUND THOSE MOUTH-WATERING SMURFS! MMM-MMM!
RUN, PAPA SMURF! RUN!
HELP!
I'VE GOT ONE!
Alas, it was written!
What? What's written?
It's written in this book that an ogre would smurf into our village to smurf all of us...
© Peyo 7

WHAT? You knew that and you didn't run away? What's the use, since it's written! You would have smurfed me in any case!

What else? Read the rest. I don't know how to read! You don't know-- Really! Hmm... uh... it's written that one hour after having eaten all the Smurfs, the ogre would smurf dead, poisoned!

POISONED? Gargamei assured me you were edible! Yes, but the Smurfs eat sarsaparilla, which is a poison for ogres!

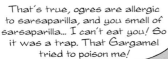

That's true, ogres are allergic to sarsaparilla, and you smell of sarsaparilla... I can't eat you! So it was a trap. That Gargamel tried to poison me!

Oh, Gargamel is the worst sort of smurf!

He'll pay for that! Show me where Gargamel lives! Follow me everyone, we'll pick him some mushrooms!

Mushrooms?

What?

Me, I don't like mushrooms!

!

That way!

?

A little later...

OPEN UP!

Who-- who's there?

It's here!

BLAM BLAM BLAM

I know you're a gourmet, that's why my friends have brought some mushrooms for the soup!

The soup? What soup?

FLLLIMP

MEOOW!

THE GOURMET'S SOUP! It's better with mushrooms! **HA, HA, HAAAAAA!** I'm hungry! Mmm-mmm!

Cursed Smurfs! I'll get revenge! **HELP!**

All's well that ends with a little party in the Smurf Village!

What? You're burning the book by Nostrasmurfus, Papa Smurf?!

Brainy Smurf, this has smurfed me that, to remain master of our smurf, it's not good knowing it in advance!

© Peyo

END

21

STRANGE SNOWMEN

Good job, Timid Smurf. Your snowman has smurfed the competition's first prize!

Really? Is that true?

Hurry up, Baby!

?

CLAP CLAP

BANG BANG

ARHOO! HEE HEE HEE!

It's not fair! We didn't finish our snowman because we're too little!

I smurf you the juniors prize!

ARHOO!

YAY!

For Snowbuddy-- HIP, HIP, HIP, HURRAY!

And tomorrow, you can all have a big snowball fight!

HEE HEE HEE!

CLAP CLAP CLAP

CLAP CLAP CLAP

!

YIPPEE

YEAH

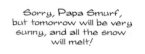

Sorry, Papa Smurf, but tomorrow will be very sunny, and all the snow will melt!

Tomorrow already?

!?

‡Sniff‡ ... I don't want my Snowbuddy to melt! I like him so much! ‡BooHooHoo‡ ... ‡sniff‡ ...

Come now, it's natural for it to melt into drops of water. They'll smurf into the river--

...and the river smurfs to the sea where the water warms--

Yes, and then the water evaporates and smurfs clouds which will smurf new snow next winter to... smurf new snowmen!

NO, I WANT TO KEEP MY SNOWBUDDY! ‡WAAH!‡

© Peyo

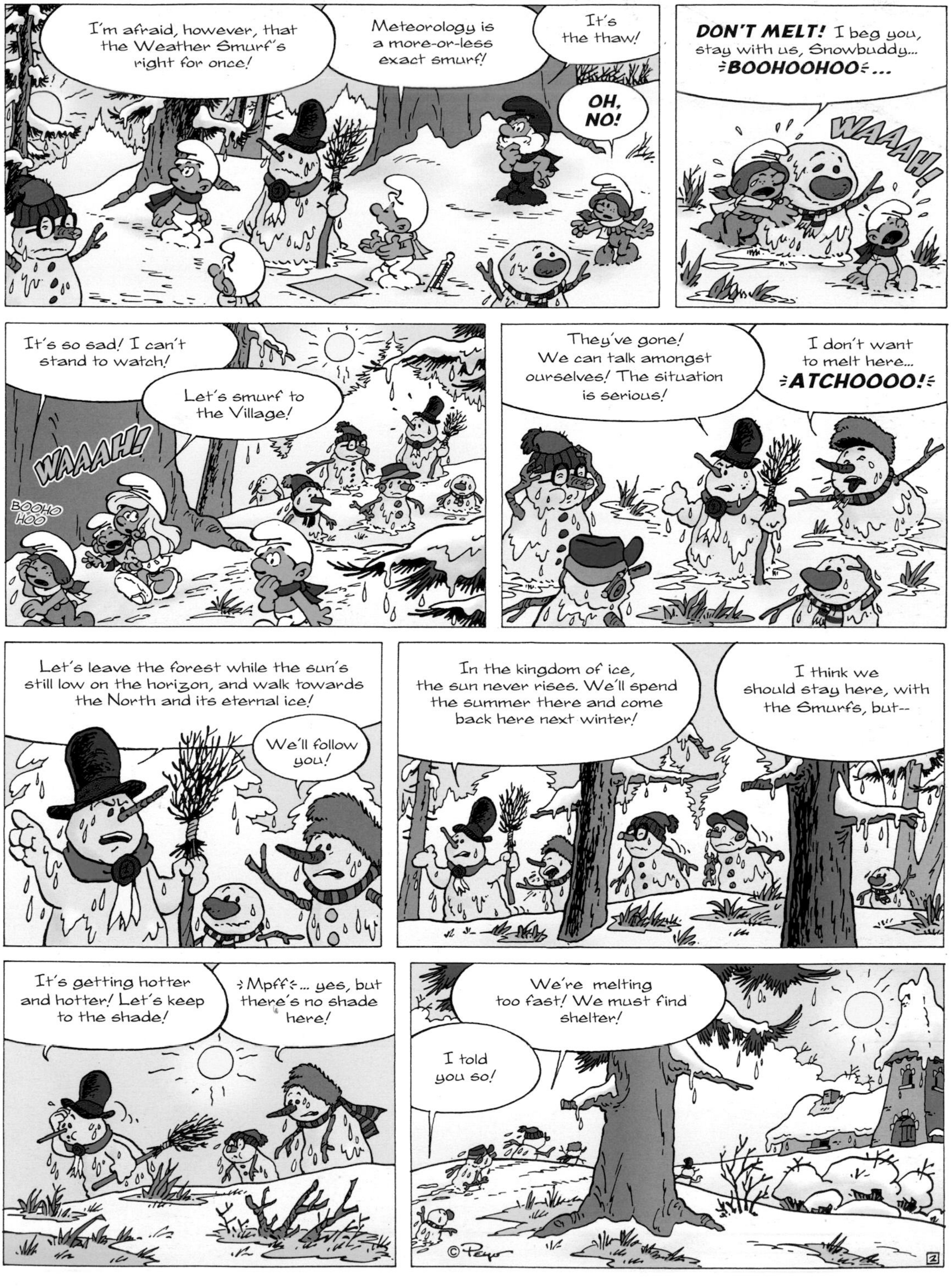
I'm afraid, however, that the Weather Smurf's right for once!
Meteorology is a more-or-less exact smurf!
It's the thaw!
OH, NO!
DON'T MELT! I beg you, stay with us, Snowbuddy... BOOHOOHOO...
WAAAH!
It's so sad! I can't stand to watch!
Let's smurf to the Village!
WAAAH!
BOOHO HOO
They've gone! We can talk amongst ourselves! The situation is serious!
I don't want to melt here... ATCHOOOO!
Let's leave the forest while the sun's still low on the horizon, and walk towards the North and its eternal ice!
We'll follow you!
In the kingdom of ice, the sun never rises. We'll spend the summer there and come back here next winter!
I think we should stay here, with the Smurfs, but--
It's getting hotter and hotter! Let's keep to the shade!
Mpff... yes, but there's no shade here!
We're melting too fast! We must find shelter!
I told you so!
© Peyo
2

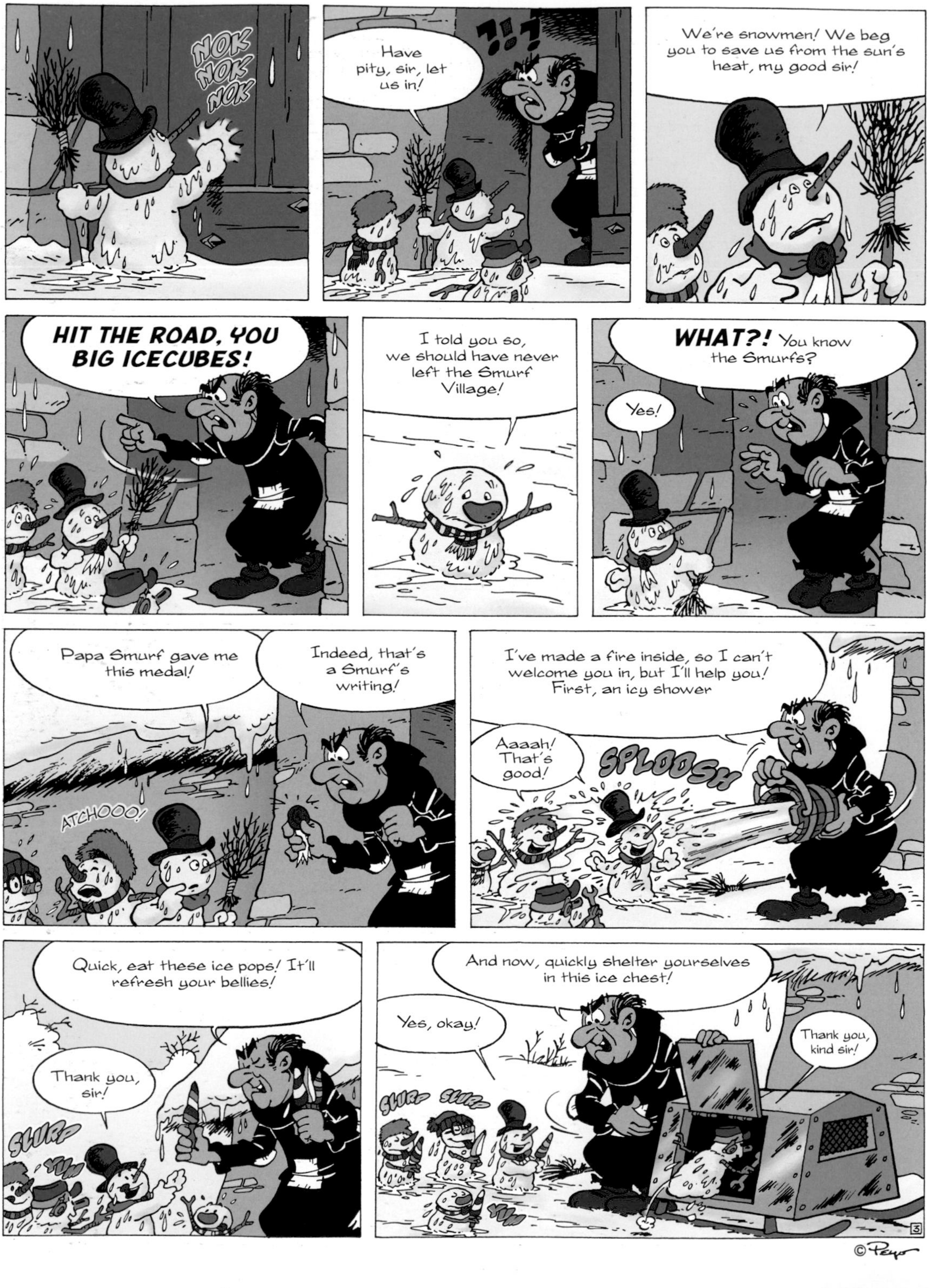
NOK NOK NOK
Have pity, sir, let us in!
?!?
We're snowmen! We beg you to save us from the sun's heat, my good sir!
HIT THE ROAD, YOU BIG ICECUBES!
I told you so, we should have never left the Smurf Village!
WHAT?! You know the Smurfs?
Yes!
Papa Smurf gave me this medal!
Indeed, that's a Smurf's writing!
ATCHOOO!
I've made a fire inside, so I can't welcome you in, but I'll help you! First, an icy shower
Aaaah! That's good!
SPLOOSH
Quick, eat these ice pops! It'll refresh your bellies!
Thank you, sir!
SLURP
YUM
And now, quickly shelter yourselves in this ice chest!
Yes, okay!
Thank you, kind sir!
SLURP SLURP
YUM
3
© Peyo

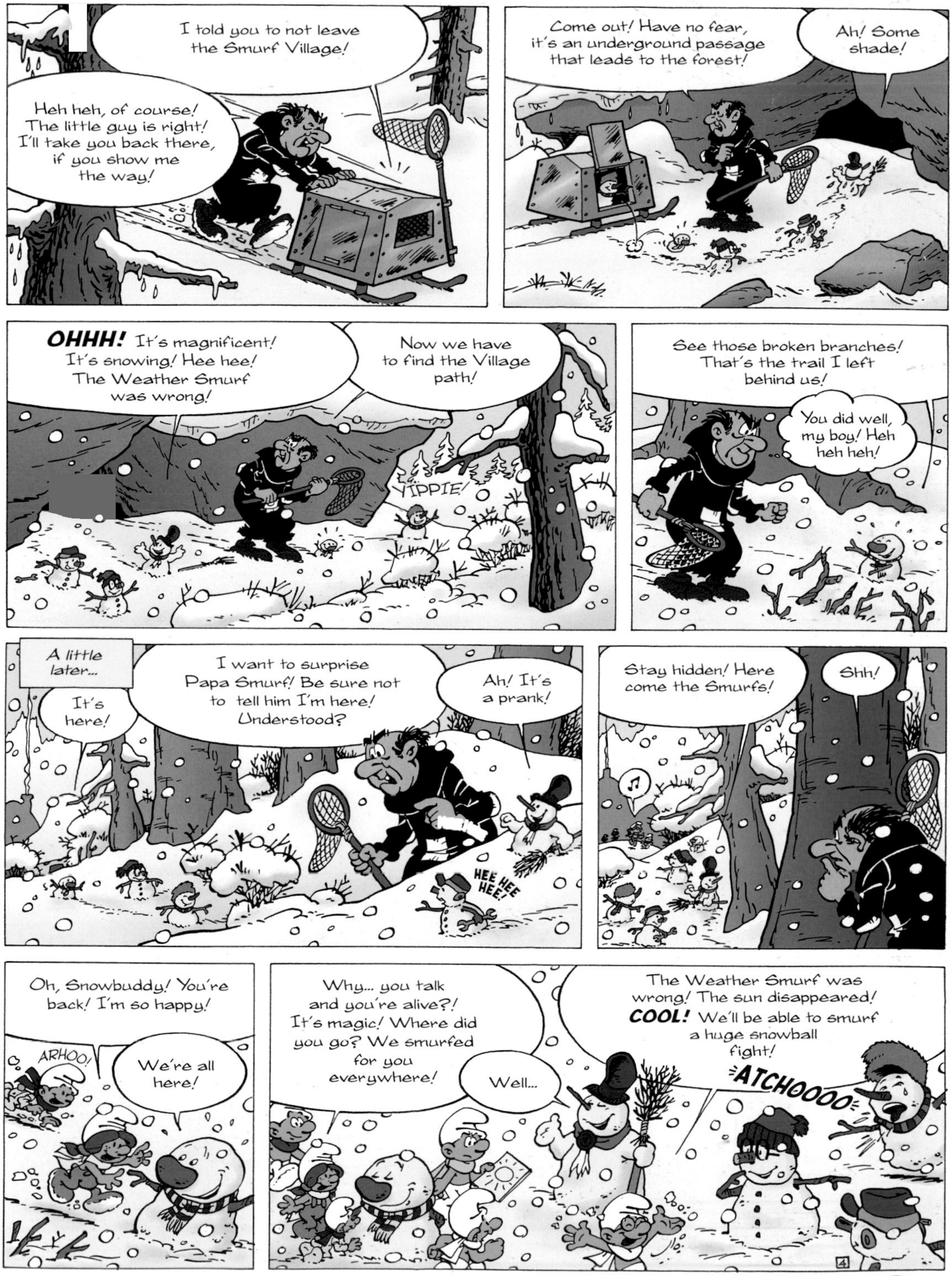
I told you to not leave the Smurf Village!
Heh heh, of course! The little guy is right! I'll take you back there, if you show me the way!
Come out! Have no fear, it's an underground passage that leads to the forest!
Ah! Some shade!
OHHH! It's magnificent! It's snowing! Hee hee! The Weather Smurf was wrong!
Now we have to find the Village path!
YIPPIE!
See those broken branches! That's the trail I left behind us!
You did well, my boy! Heh heh heh!
A little later...
It's here!
I want to surprise Papa Smurf! Be sure not to tell him I'm here! Understood?
Ah! It's a prank!
HEE HEE HEE!
Stay hidden! Here come the Smurfs!
Shh!
Oh, Snowbuddy! You're back! I'm so happy!
ARHOO!
We're all here!
Why... you talk and you're alive?! It's magic! Where did you go? We smurfed for you everywhere!
Well...
The Weather Smurf was wrong! The sun disappeared! COOL! We'll be able to smurf a huge snowball fight!
ATCHOOOO

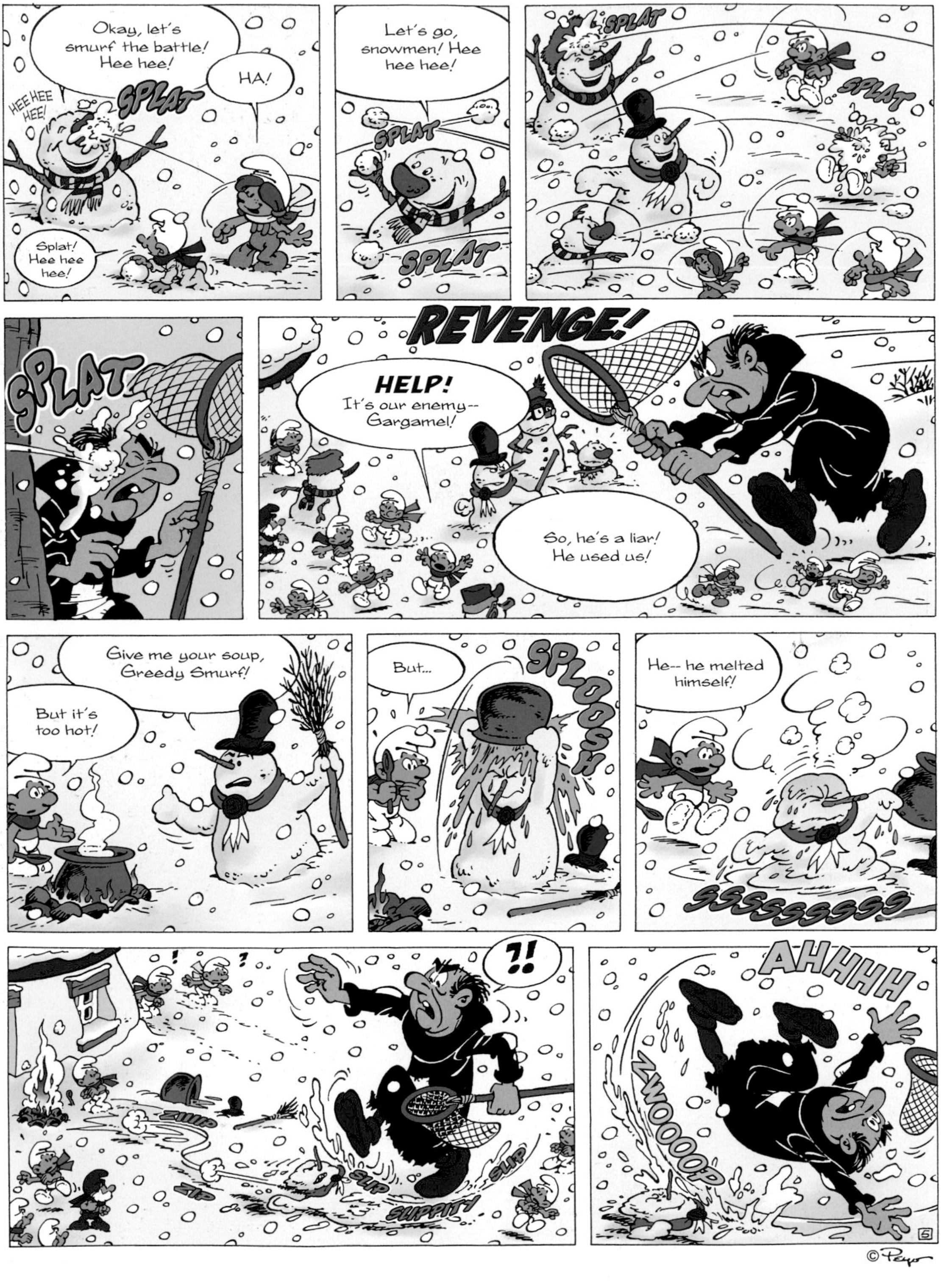
Okay, let's smurf the battle! Hee hee!
HA!
HEE HEE HEE!
SPLAT
Splat! Hee hee hee!
Let's go, snowmen! Hee hee hee!
SPLAT
SPLAT
SPLAT
SPLAT
SPLAT
SPLAT
REVENGE!
HELP!
It's our enemy-- Gargamel!
So, he's a liar! He used us!
Give me your soup, Greedy Smurf!
But it's too hot!
But...
SPLOOOSH
He-- he melted himself!
SSSSSSSSS
?!
ZIIIP
ZIP
SLIP
SLIP
SLIPPITY
AHHHH
ZWOOOOP
5
© Peyo

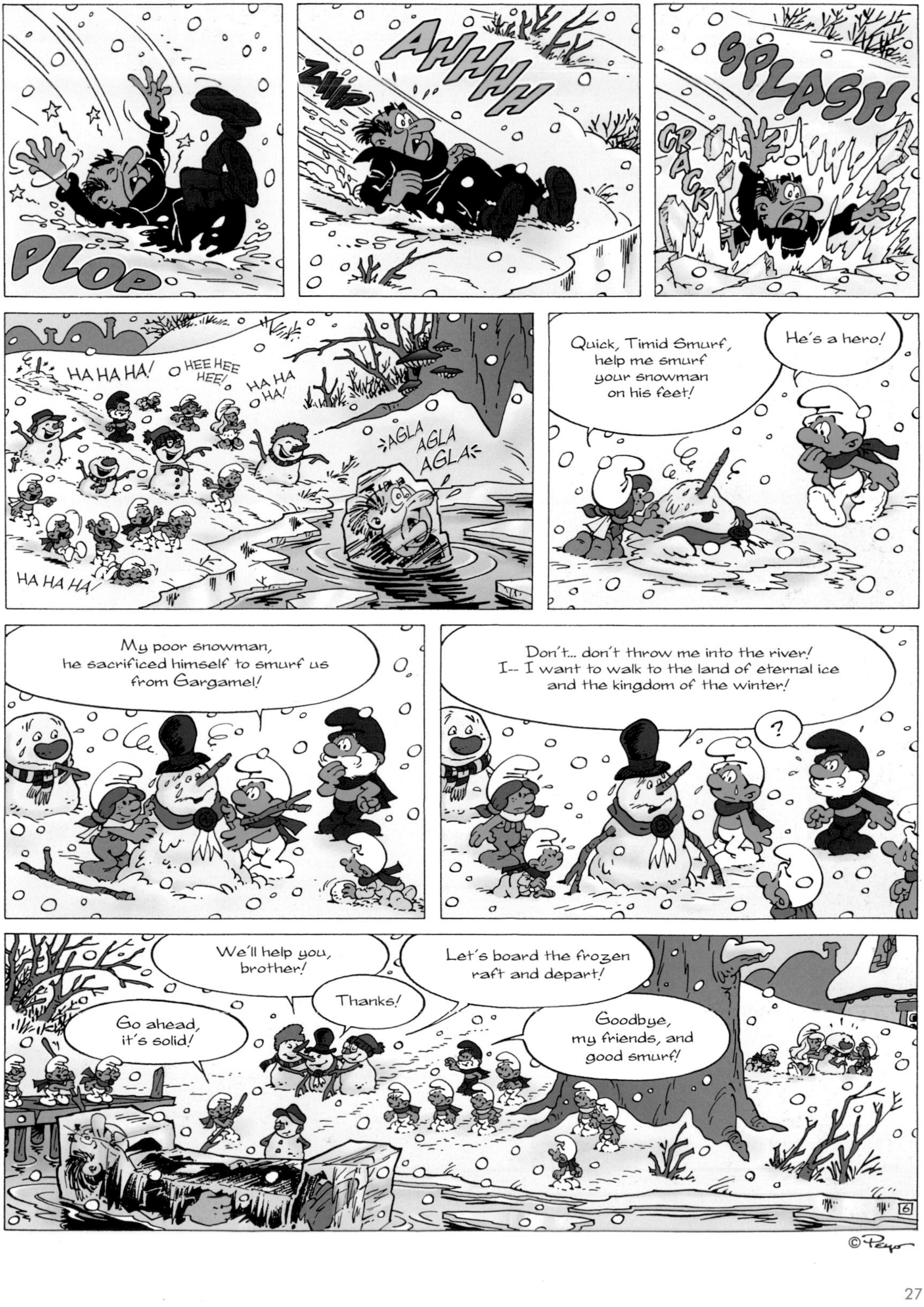
PLOP
ZIIIP
AHHHH
SPLASH
CRACK
HA HA HA!
HEE HEE HEE!
HA HA HA!
AGLA AGLA AGLA
HA HA HA!
Quick, Timid Smurf, help me smurf your snowman on his feet!
He's a hero!
My poor snowman, he sacrificed himself to smurf us from Gargamel!
Don't... don't throw me into the river! I-- I want to walk to the land of eternal ice and the kingdom of the winter!
?
We'll help you, brother!
Let's board the frozen raft and depart!
Thanks!
Go ahead, it's solid!
Goodbye, my friends, and good smurf!
6

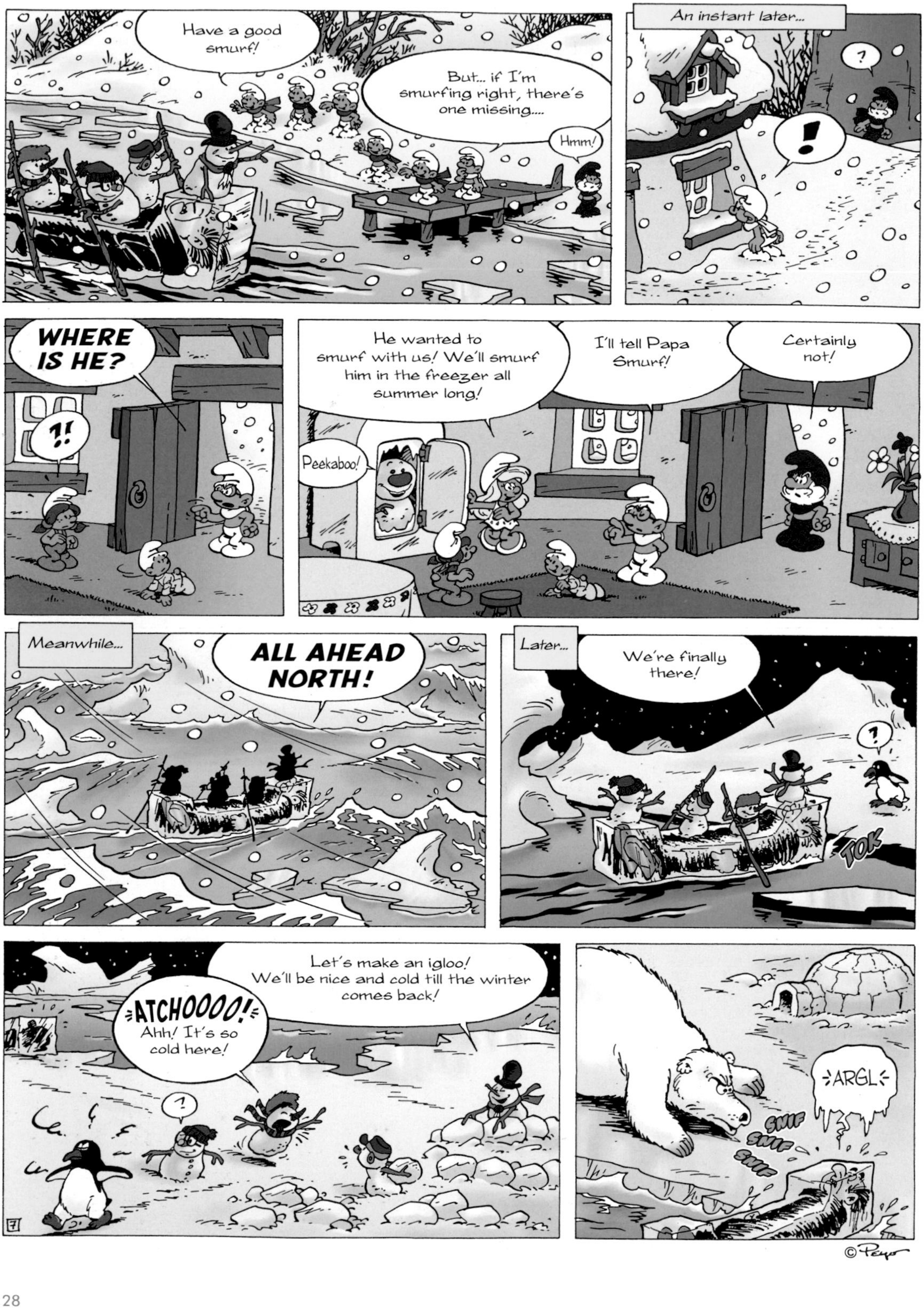
Have a good smurf!
But... if I'm smurfing right, there's one missing....
Hmm!
An instant later...
?
!
WHERE IS HE?
?!
He wanted to smurf with us! We'll smurf him in the freezer all summer long!
Peekaboo!
I'll tell Papa Smurf!
Certainly not!
Meanwhile...
ALL AHEAD NORTH!
Later...
We're finally there!
?
TOK
Let's make an igloo! We'll be nice and cold till the winter comes back!
ATCHOOOO! Ahh! It's so cold here!
?
ARGL
SNIF
SNIF
SNIF
7
© Peyo

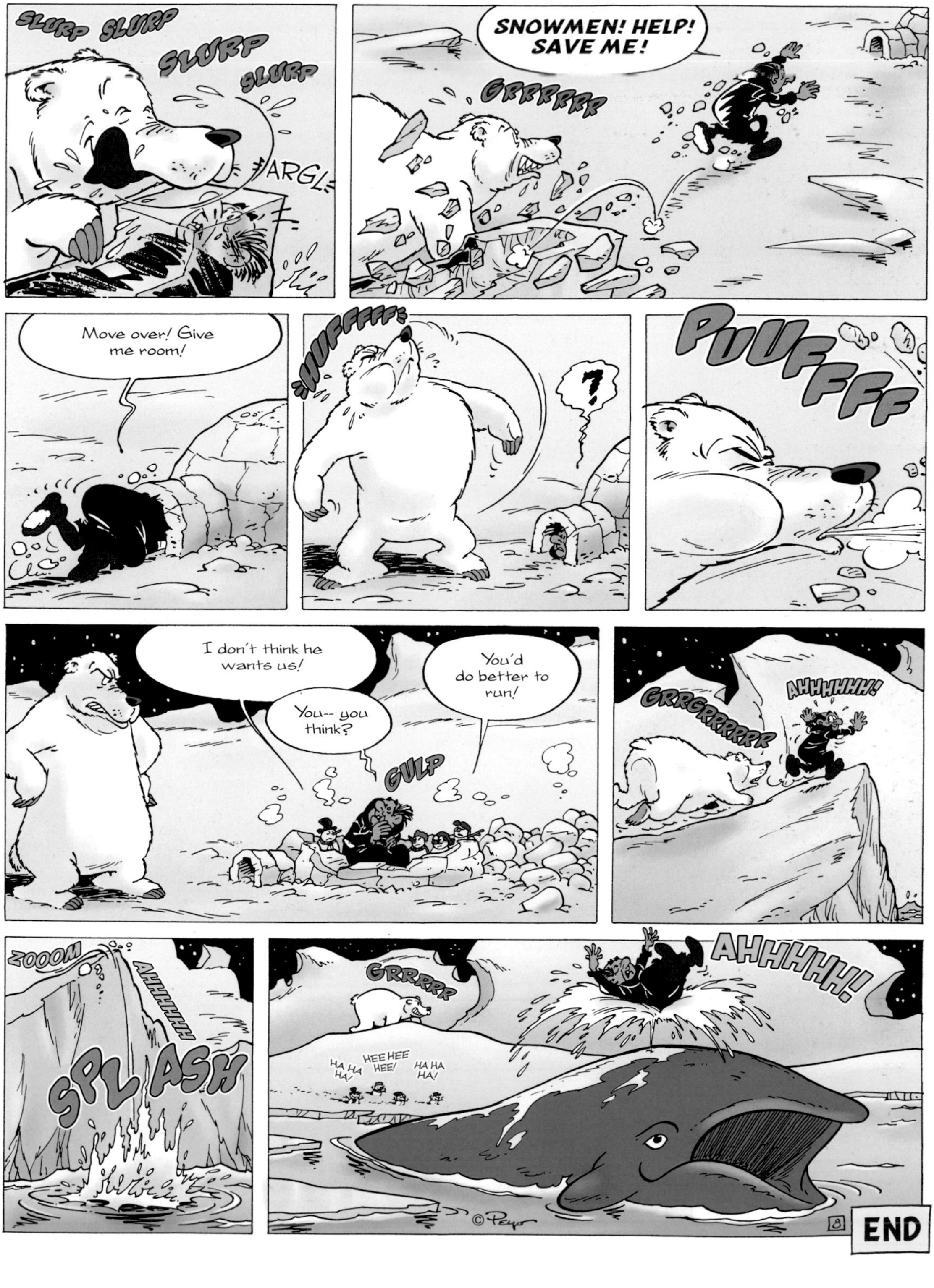

SLURP SLURP
SLURP
SLURP
ARGL
SNOWMEN! HELP! SAVE ME!
GRRRRRR
Move over! Give me room!
HUFFFFFF
?
PUUFFFFF
I don't think he wants us!
You'd do better to run!
You-- you think?
GULP
GRRRGRRRRRR
AHHHHHH!
ZOOOM
AHHHHHH
SPLASH
GRRRRR
AHHHHHH!
HA HA HA!
HEE HEE HEE!
HA HA HA!
© Peyo
8

END

HIBERNATUS SMURFIMUS

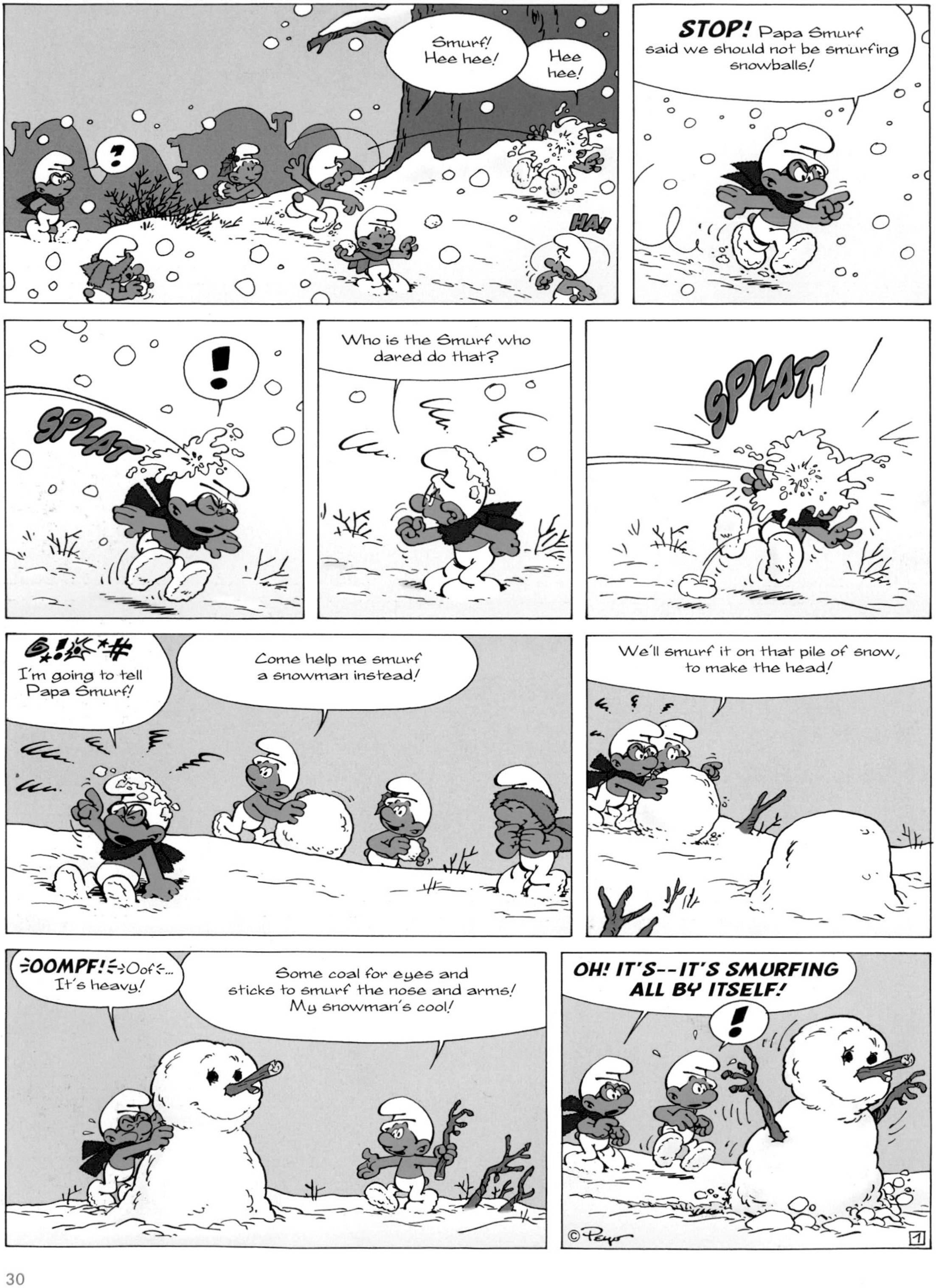

Smurf! Hee hee!
Hee hee!
?
HA!
STOP! Papa Smurf said we should not be smurfing snowballs!
!
SPLAT
Who is the Smurf who dared do that?
SPLAT
G!*#
I'm going to tell Papa Smurf!
Come help me smurf a snowman instead!
We'll smurf it on that pile of snow, to make the head!
OOMPF! Oof... It's heavy!
Some coal for eyes and sticks to smurf the nose and arms! My snowman's cool!
OH! IT'S--IT'S SMURFING ALL BY ITSELF!
!
© Peyo
1

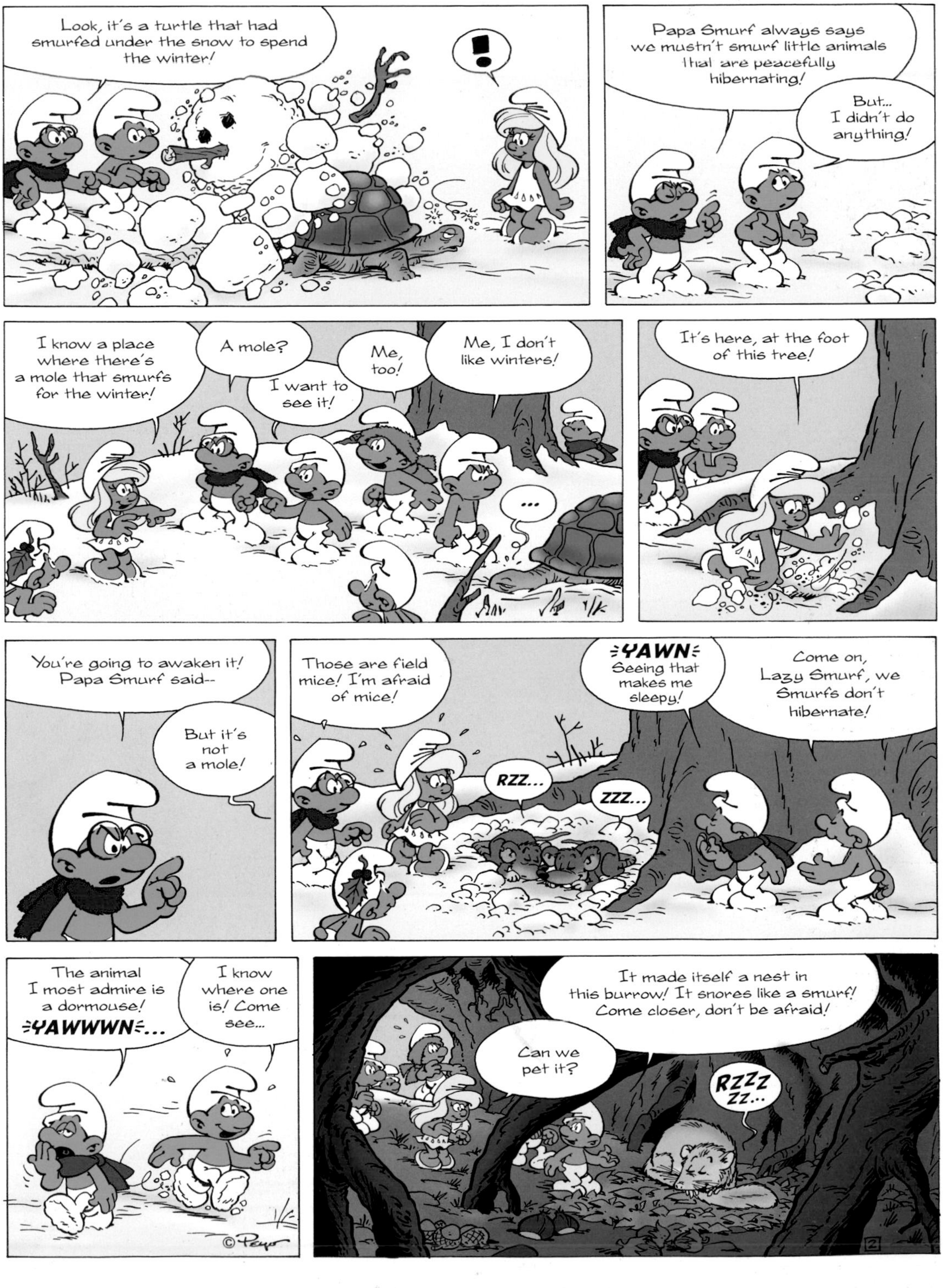
Look, it's a turtle that had smurfed under the snow to spend the winter!
!
Papa Smurf always says we mustn't smurf little animals that are peacefully hibernating!
But... I didn't do anything!
I know a place where there's a mole that smurfs for the winter!
A mole?
I want to see it!
Me, too!
Me, I don't like winters!
...
It's here, at the foot of this tree!
You're going to awaken it! Papa Smurf said--
But it's not a mole!
Those are field mice! I'm afraid of mice!
RZZ...
ZZZ...
YAWN Seeing that makes me sleepy!
Come on, Lazy Smurf, we Smurfs don't hibernate!
The animal I most admire is a dormouse! YAWWWN...
I know where one is! Come see...
It made itself a nest in this burrow! It snores like a smurf! Come closer, don't be afraid!
Can we pet it?
RZZZ ZZ...
© Peyo

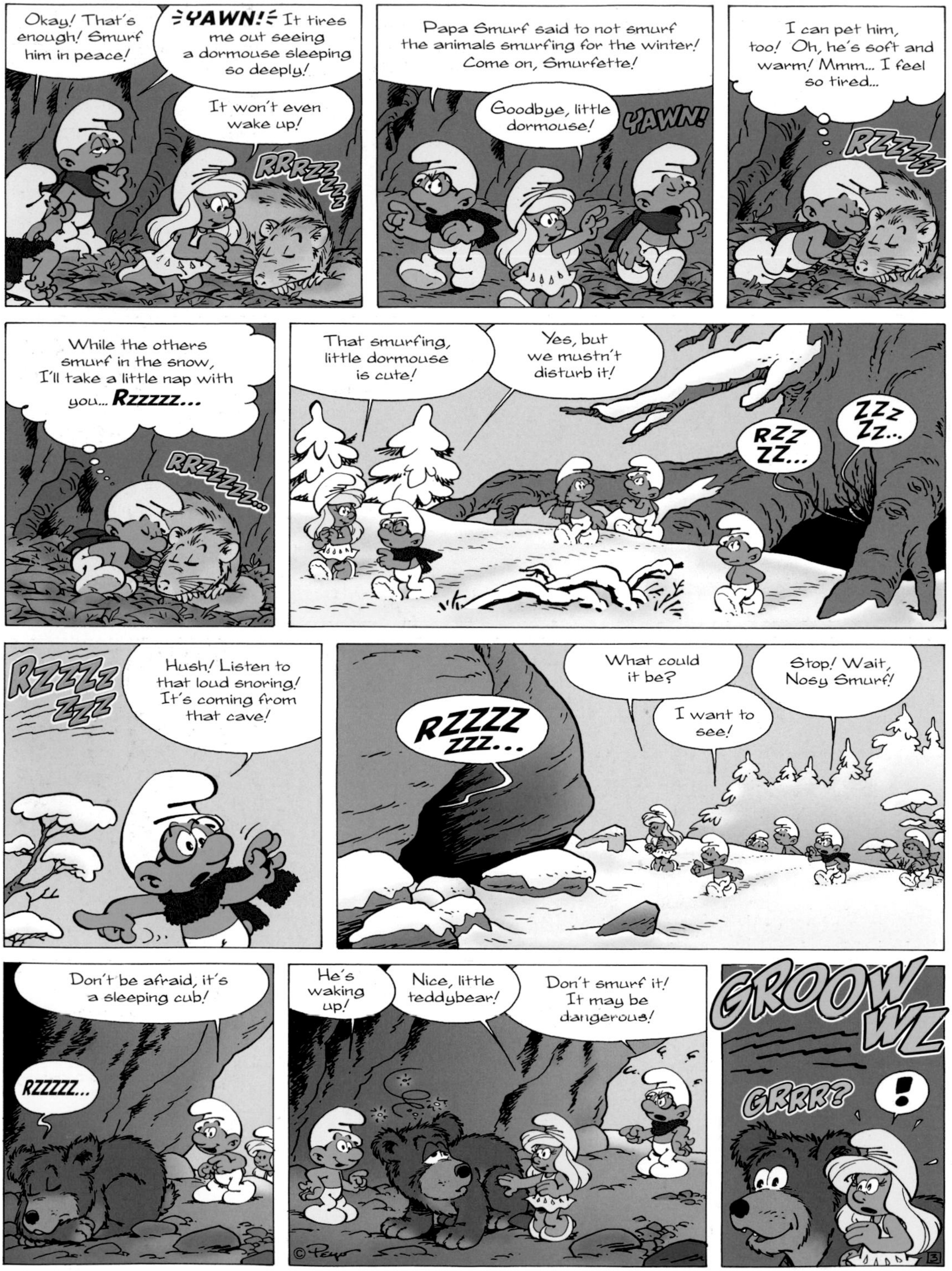
Okay! That's enough! Smurf him in peace!
YAWN! It tires me out seeing a dormouse sleeping so deeply!
It won't even wake up!
RRRZZZZZ
Papa Smurf said to not smurf the animals smurfing for the winter! Come on, Smurfette!
Goodbye, little dormouse!
YAWN!
I can pet him, too! Oh, he's soft and warm! Mmm... I feel so tired...
RZZZZZZ
While the others smurf in the snow, I'll take a little nap with you... Rzzzzz...
RRZZZZZZZ...
That smurfing, little dormouse is cute!
Yes, but we mustn't disturb it!
RZZ ZZ...
ZZZ ZZ...
RZZZZ ZZZ
Hush! Listen to that loud snoring! It's coming from that cave!
RZZZZ ZZZ...
What could it be?
I want to see!
Stop! Wait, Nosy Smurf!
Don't be afraid, it's a sleeping cub!
RZZZZZ...
He's waking up!
Nice, little teddybear!
Don't smurf it! It may be dangerous!
© Peyo
GROOWWL
GRRR?
!
3

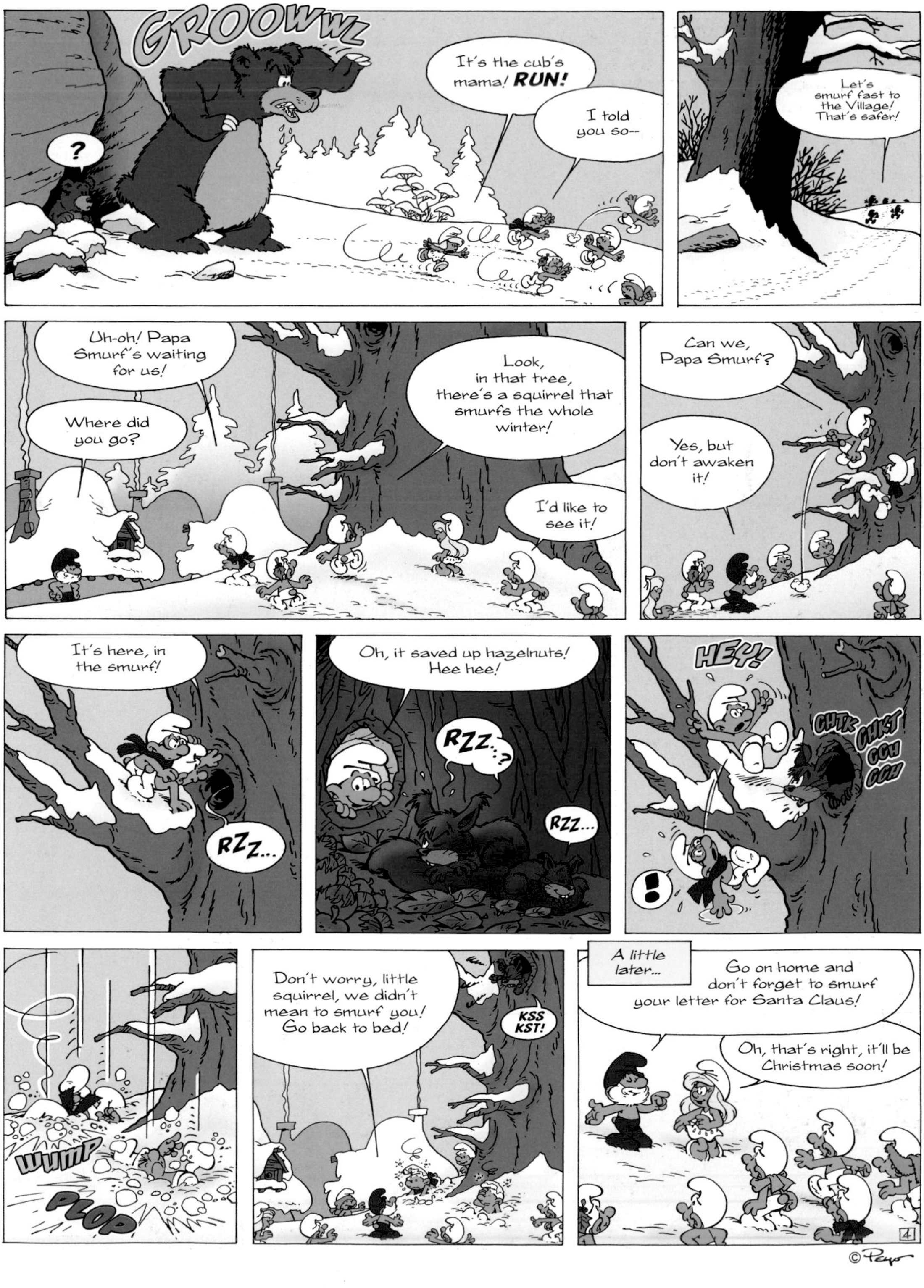
GROOWWL
?
It's the cub's mama! RUN!
I told you so--
Let's smurf fast to the Village! That's safer!
Uh-oh! Papa Smurf's waiting for us!
Where did you go?
Look, in that tree, there's a squirrel that smurfs the whole winter!
I'd like to see it!
Can we, Papa Smurf?
Yes, but don't awaken it!
It's here, in the smurf!
RZZ...
Oh, it saved up hazelnuts! Hee hee!
RZZ...?
RZZ...
HEY!
CHTK CHKT CCH CCH
!
WUMP
PLOP
Don't worry, little squirrel, we didn't mean to smurf you! Go back to bed!
KSS KST!
A little later...
Go on home and don't forget to smurf your letter for Santa Claus!
Oh, that's right, it'll be Christmas soon!
4
© Peyo

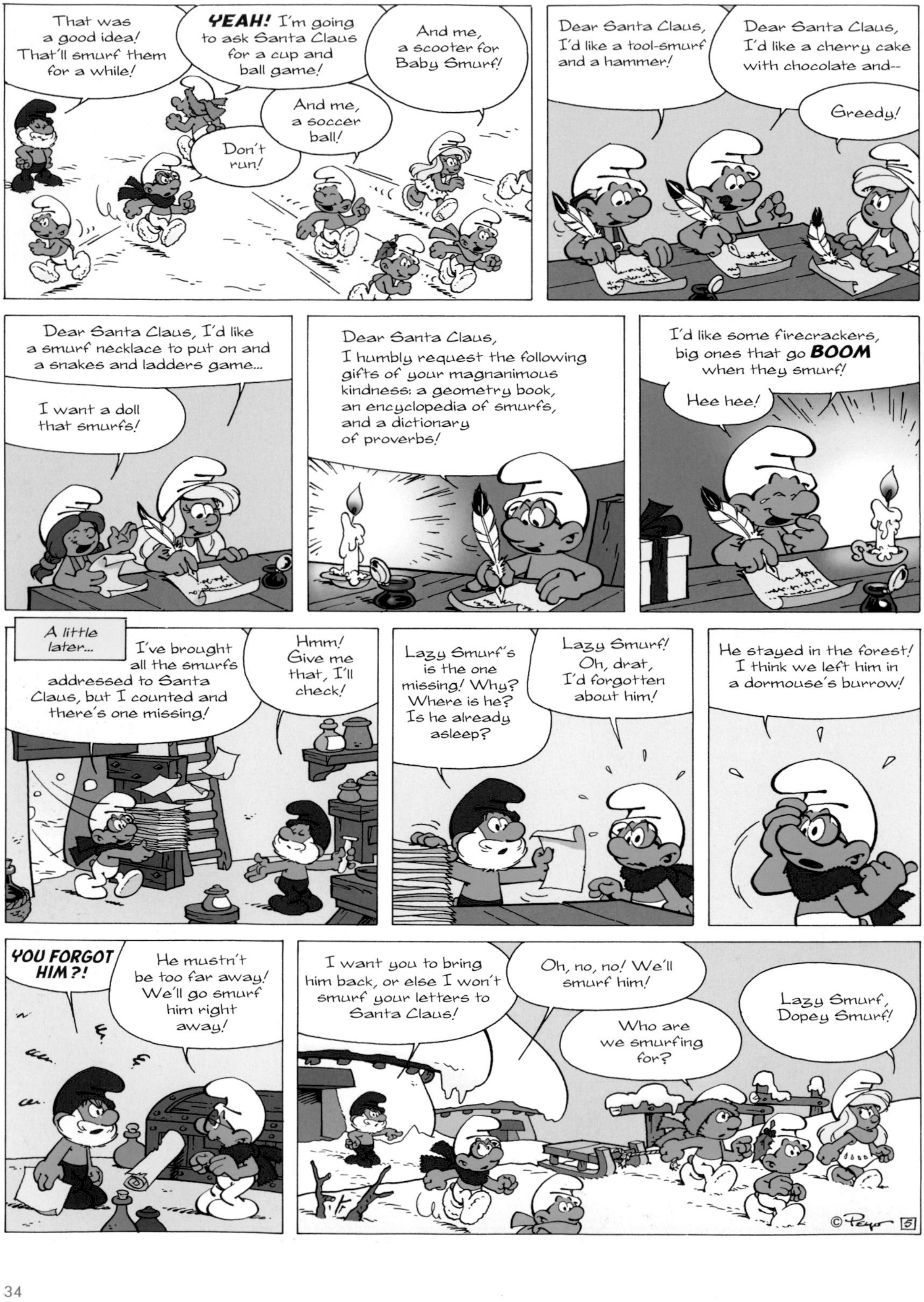
That was a good idea! That'll smurf them for a while!
YEAH! I'm going to ask Santa Claus for a cup and ball game!
And me, a scooter for Baby Smurf!
And me, a soccer ball!
Don't run!
Dear Santa Claus, I'd like a tool-smurf and a hammer!
Dear Santa Claus, I'd like a cherry cake with chocolate and--
Greedy!
Dear Santa Claus, I'd like a smurf necklace to put on and a snakes and ladders game...
I want a doll that smurfs!
Dear Santa Claus, I humbly request the following gifts of your magnanimous kindness: a geometry book, an encyclopedia of smurfs, and a dictionary of proverbs!
I'd like some firecrackers, big ones that go BOOM when they smurf!
Hee hee!
A little later...
I've brought all the smurfs addressed to Santa Claus, but I counted and there's one missing!
Hmm! Give me that, I'll check!
Lazy Smurf's is the one missing! Why? Where is he? Is he already asleep?
Lazy Smurf! Oh, drat, I'd forgotten about him!
He stayed in the forest! I think we left him in a dormouse's burrow!
YOU FORGOT HIM?!
He mustn't be too far away! We'll go smurf him right away!
I want you to bring him back, or else I won't smurf your letters to Santa Claus!
Oh, no, no! We'll smurf him!
Who are we smurfing for?
Lazy Smurf, Dopey Smurf!
© Peyo 5

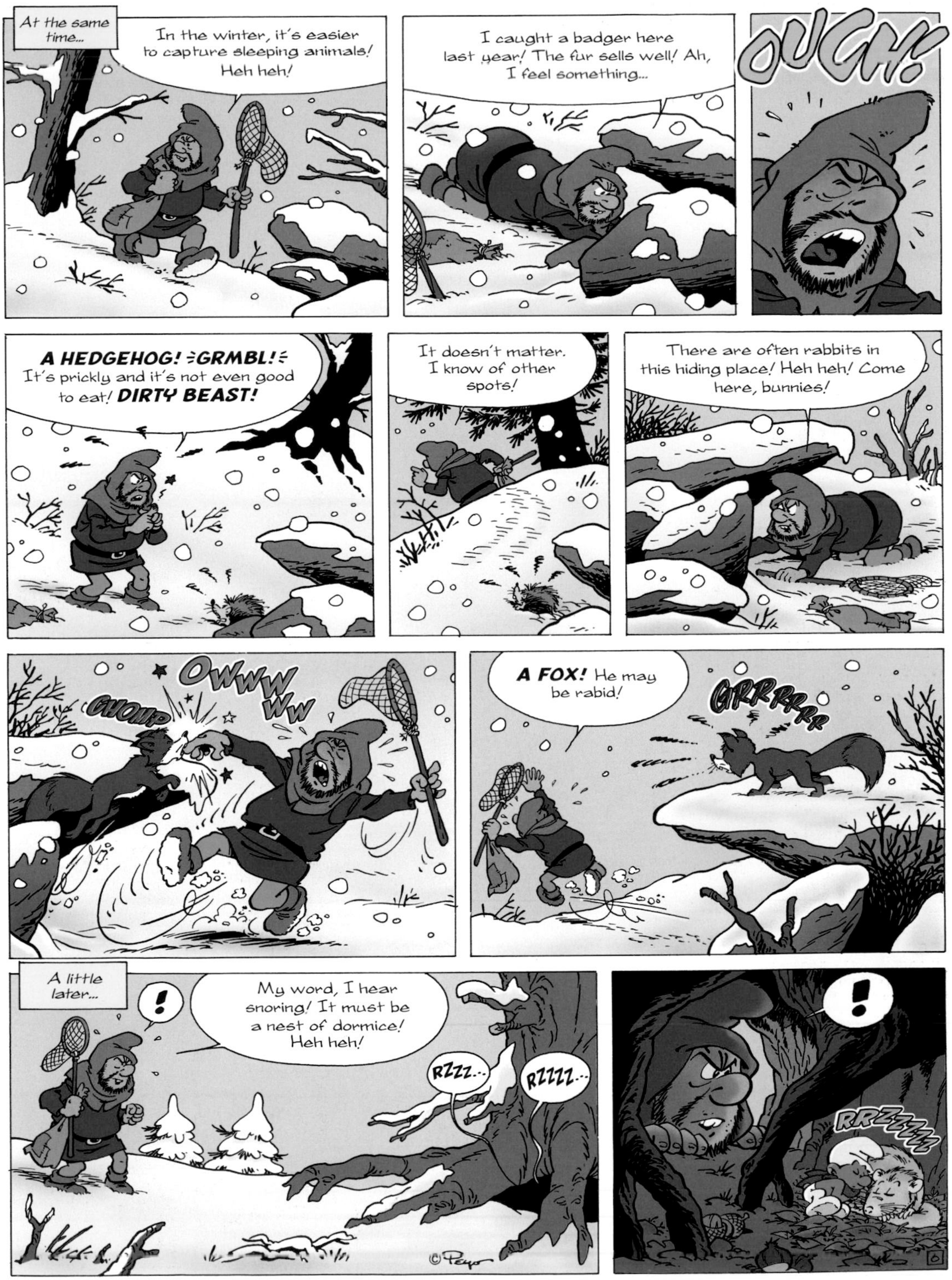
At the same time...
In the winter, it's easier to capture sleeping animals! Heh heh!
I caught a badger here last year! The fur sells well! Ah, I feel something...
OUCH!
A HEDGEHOG! GRMBL! It's prickly and it's not even good to eat! DIRTY BEAST!
It doesn't matter. I know of other spots!
There are often rabbits in this hiding place! Heh heh! Come here, bunnies!
CHOMP
OWWWWWW
A FOX! He may be rabid!
GRRRRRRR
A little later...
!
My word, I hear snoring! It must be a nest of dormice! Heh heh!
RZZZ...
RZZZZ...
©Peyo
!
RRZZZZZ

A Smurf and a dormouse! Heh heh! Good catch! They haven't even woken up! The dormouse is for me, but I know Gargamel will give me two gold coins for the Smurf!

RZZZ RZZZZZ

YOO-HOO! Where are you, Lazy Smurf? It's us!

The snow hasn't smurfed our tracks yet! Maybe he stayed with the dormouse under that tree!

Five more Smurfs! Hee hee! It's my lucky day!

Careful, there are human tracks here! It's dangerous!

DARN! They're going to escape me! I must act fast!

RZ...

⇥RHAAA!⇤ I WANT ALL OF YOU! HA, HA, HAAA!

Eeeeee! It's a wicked smurf!

RZ... RZ...

Run for your smurfs!

Help us, little smurf!

!

We're being chased by a mean smurf!

GRRR?!

HA HA! I'VE GOT YOU!

RZZz RZz

GGRROOWL!

© Peyo

Did you see?! That bandit has captured Lazy Smurf and the little dormouse!

HELP!

GGRROOWL!

GRT GRT GRK

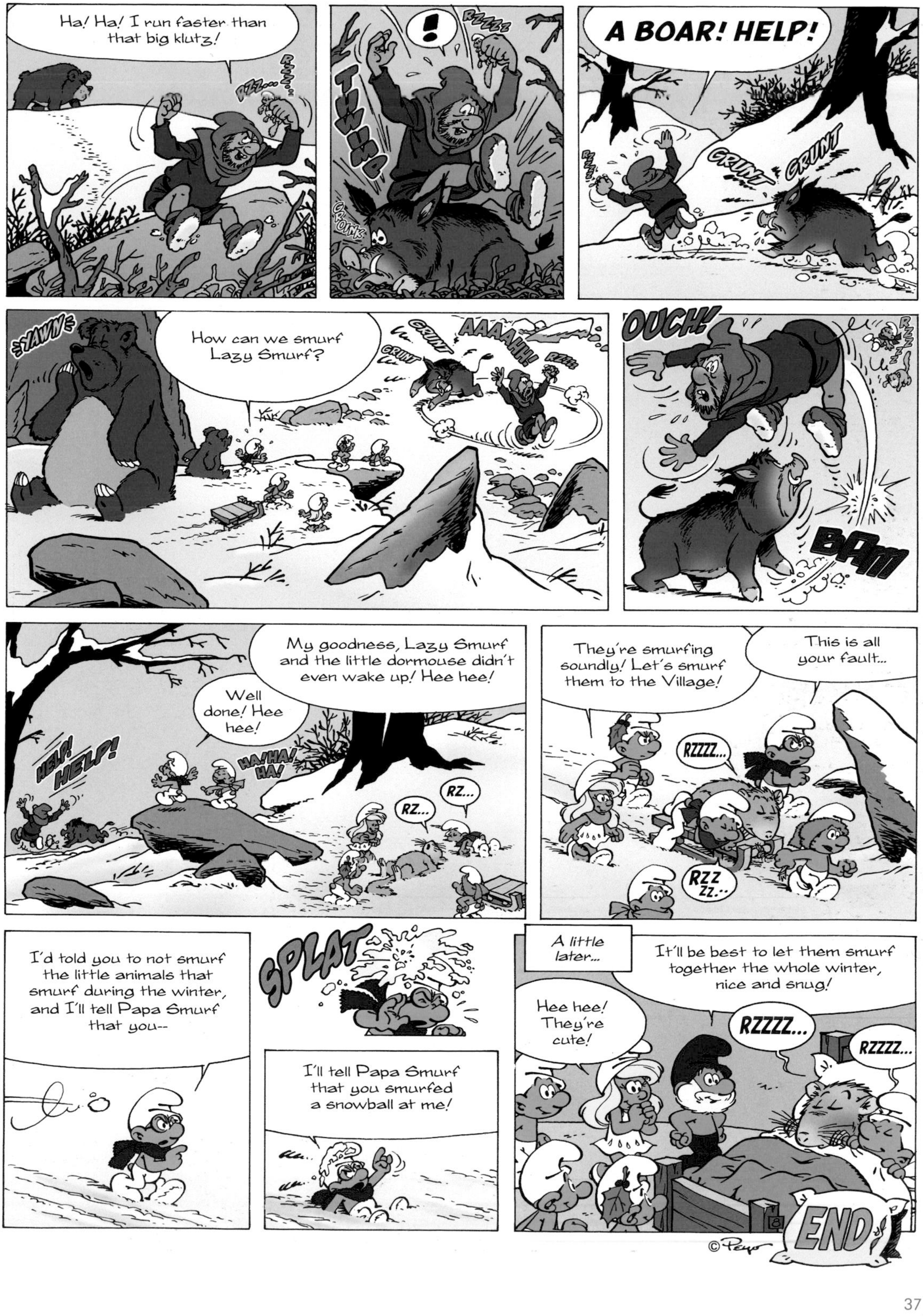
Ha! Ha! I run faster than that big klutz!
RZZZ...
!
RZZZZ
TWHMG
GROUNK
A BOAR! HELP!
GRUNT
GRUNT
YAWN
How can we smurf Lazy Smurf?
GRUNT
GRUNT
AAAAHH!
OUCH!
BAM
My goodness, Lazy Smurf and the little dormouse didn't even wake up! Hee hee!
Well done! Hee hee!
HELP! HELP!
HA! HA! HA!
RZ...
RZ...
They're smurfing soundly! Let's smurf them to the Village!
This is all your fault...
RZZZZ...
RZZ ZZ...
I'd told you to not smurf the little animals that smurf during the winter, and I'll tell Papa Smurf that you--
SPLAT
I'll tell Papa Smurf that you smurfed a snowball at me!
A little later...
It'll be best to let them smurf together the whole winter, nice and snug!
Hee hee! They're cute!
RZZZZ...
RZZZZ...
END
© Peyo

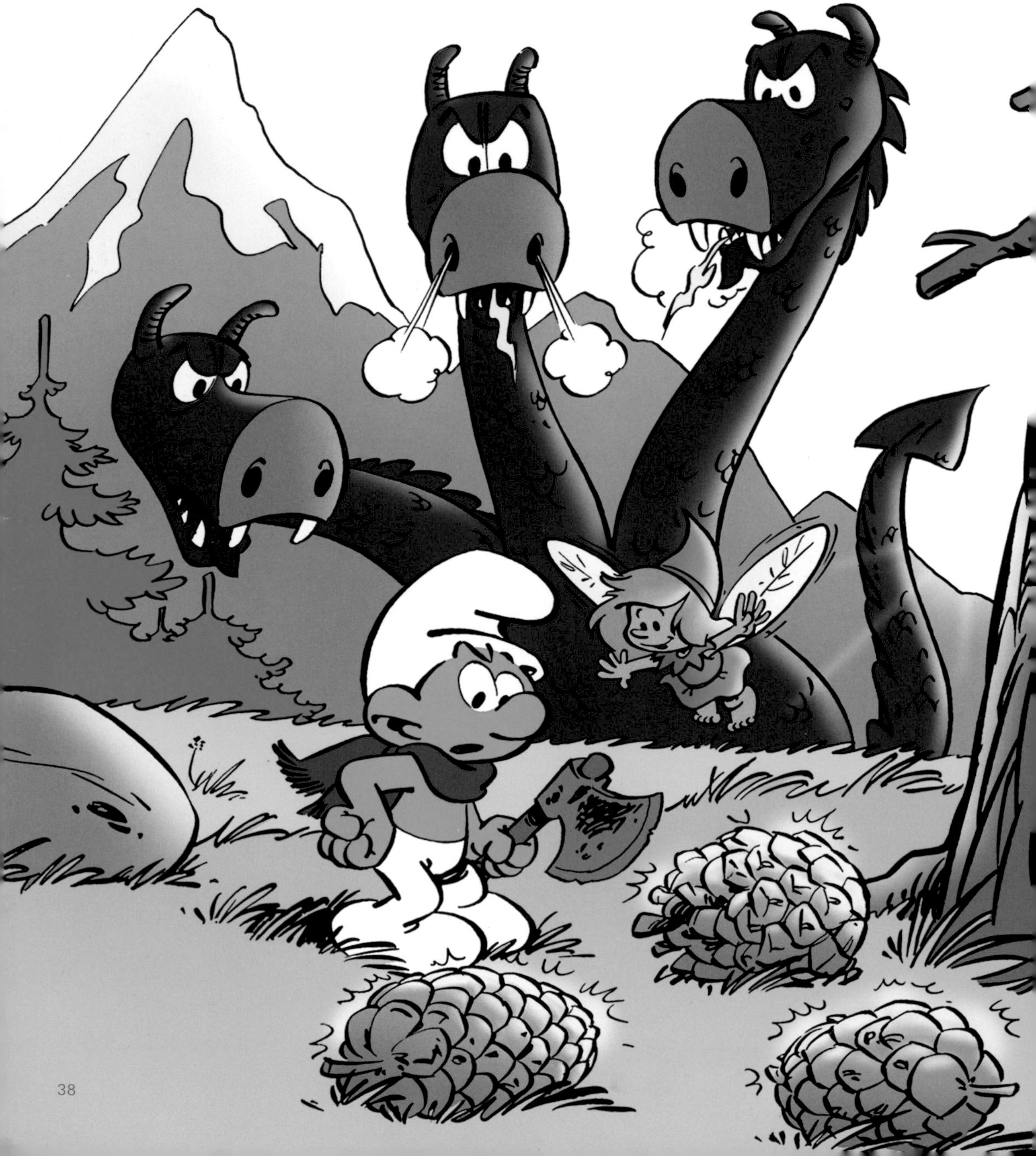

THE LITTLE TREE

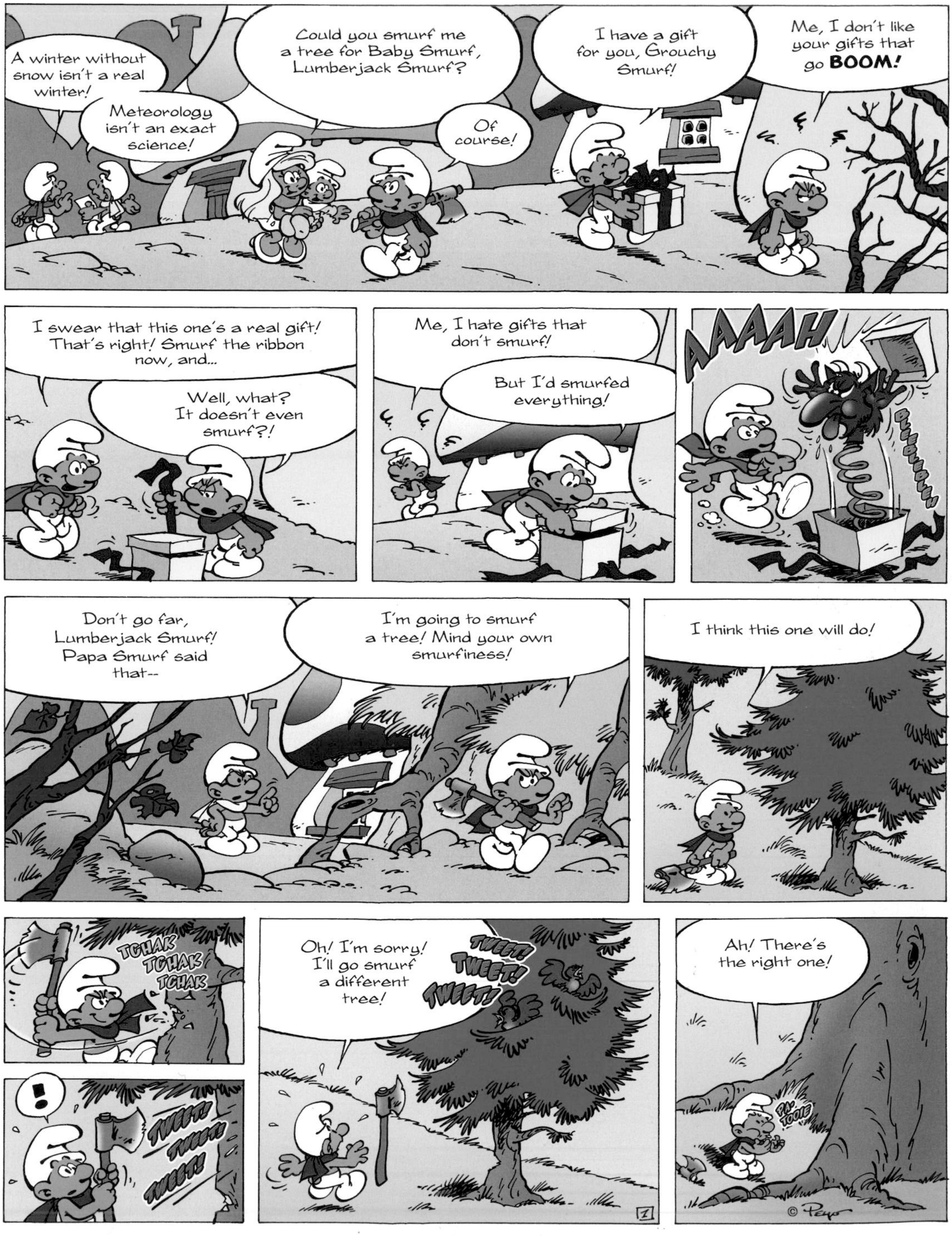
A winter without snow isn't a real winter!
Meteorology isn't an exact science!
Could you smurf me a tree for Baby Smurf, Lumberjack Smurf?
Of course!
I have a gift for you, Grouchy Smurf!
Me, I don't like your gifts that go BOOM!
I swear that this one's a real gift! That's right! Smurf the ribbon now, and...
Well, what? It doesn't even smurf?!
Me, I hate gifts that don't smurf!
But I'd smurfed everything!
AAAAH
Don't go far, Lumberjack Smurf! Papa Smurf said that--
I'm going to smurf a tree! Mind your own smurfiness!
I think this one will do!
TCHAK TCHAK TCHAK
!
TWEET! TWEET! TWEET!
Oh! I'm sorry! I'll go smurf a different tree!
TWEET! TWEET! TWEET!
Ah! There's the right one!
PA-TOOIE
1
© Peyo

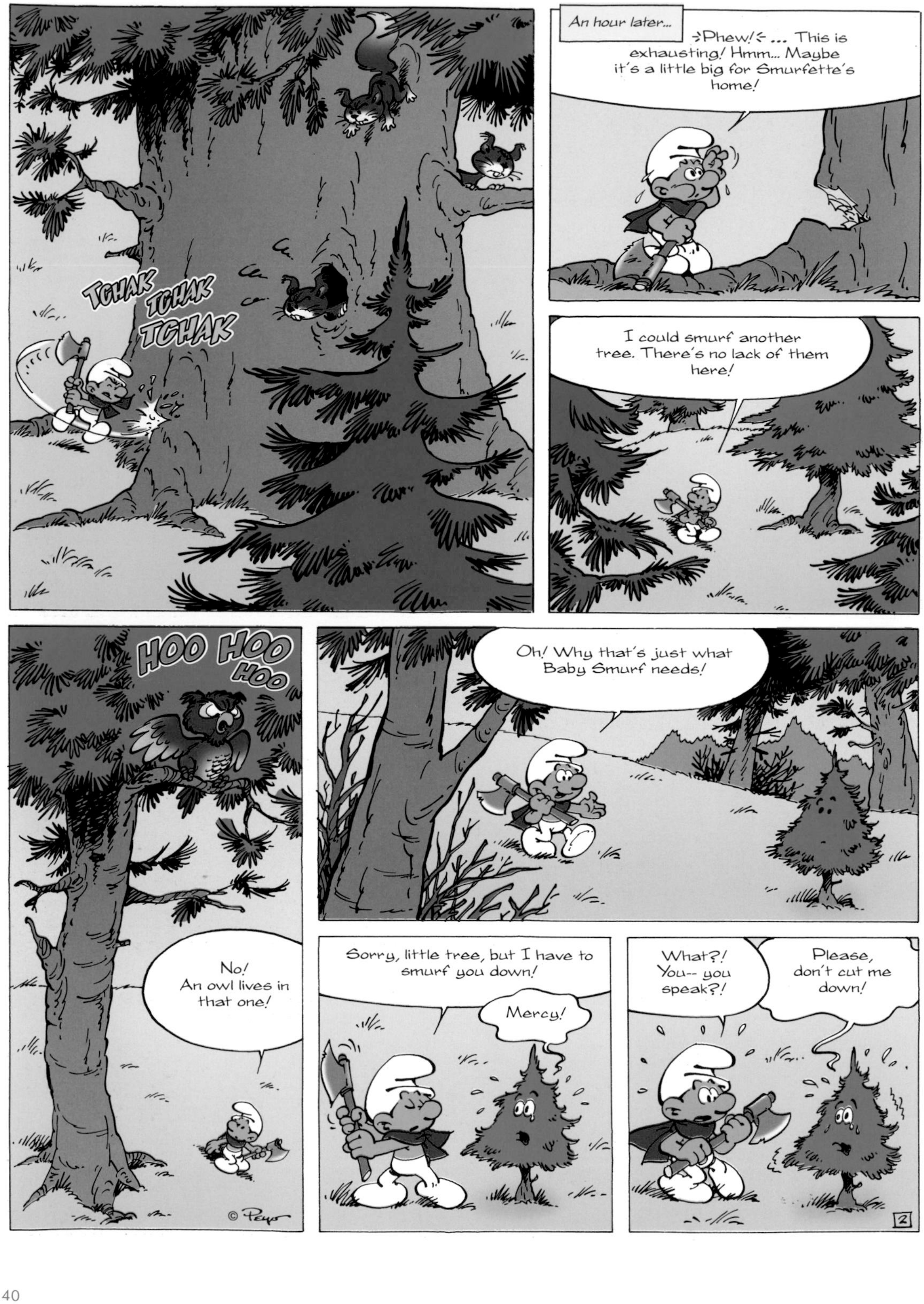
TCHAK TCHAK TCHAK
An hour later...
Phew! ... This is exhausting! Hmm... Maybe it's a little big for Smurfette's home!
I could smurf another tree. There's no lack of them here!
HOO HOO HOO
No! An owl lives in that one!
Oh! Why that's just what Baby Smurf needs!
Sorry, little tree, but I have to smurf you down!
Mercy!
What?! You-- you speak?!
Please, don't cut me down!
© Peyo
2

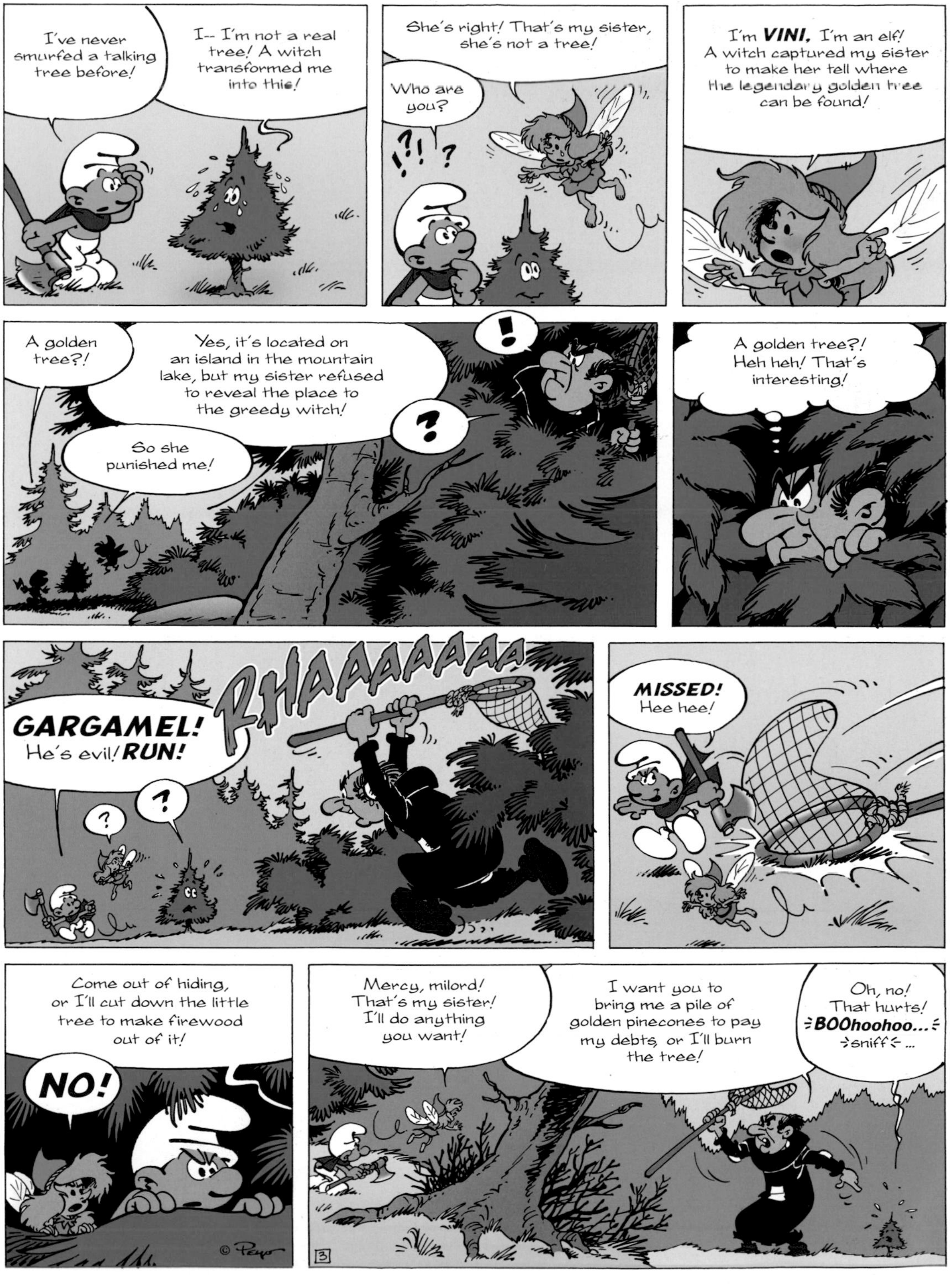
I've never smurfed a talking tree before!
I-- I'm not a real tree! A witch transformed me into this!
She's right! That's my sister, she's not a tree!
Who are you?
?!! ?
I'm VINI, I'm an elf! A witch captured my sister to make her tell where the legendary golden tree can be found!
A golden tree?!
Yes, it's located on an island in the mountain lake, but my sister refused to reveal the place to the greedy witch!
So she punished me!
!
?
A golden tree?! Heh heh! That's interesting!
GARGAMEL! He's evil! RUN!
RHAAAAAAAA
?
?
MISSED! Hee hee!
Come out of hiding, or I'll cut down the little tree to make firewood out of it!
NO!
© Peyo
Mercy, milord! That's my sister! I'll do anything you want!
I want you to bring me a pile of golden pinecones to pay my debts, or I'll burn the tree!
Oh, no! That hurts! BOOhoohoo... sniff ...
3

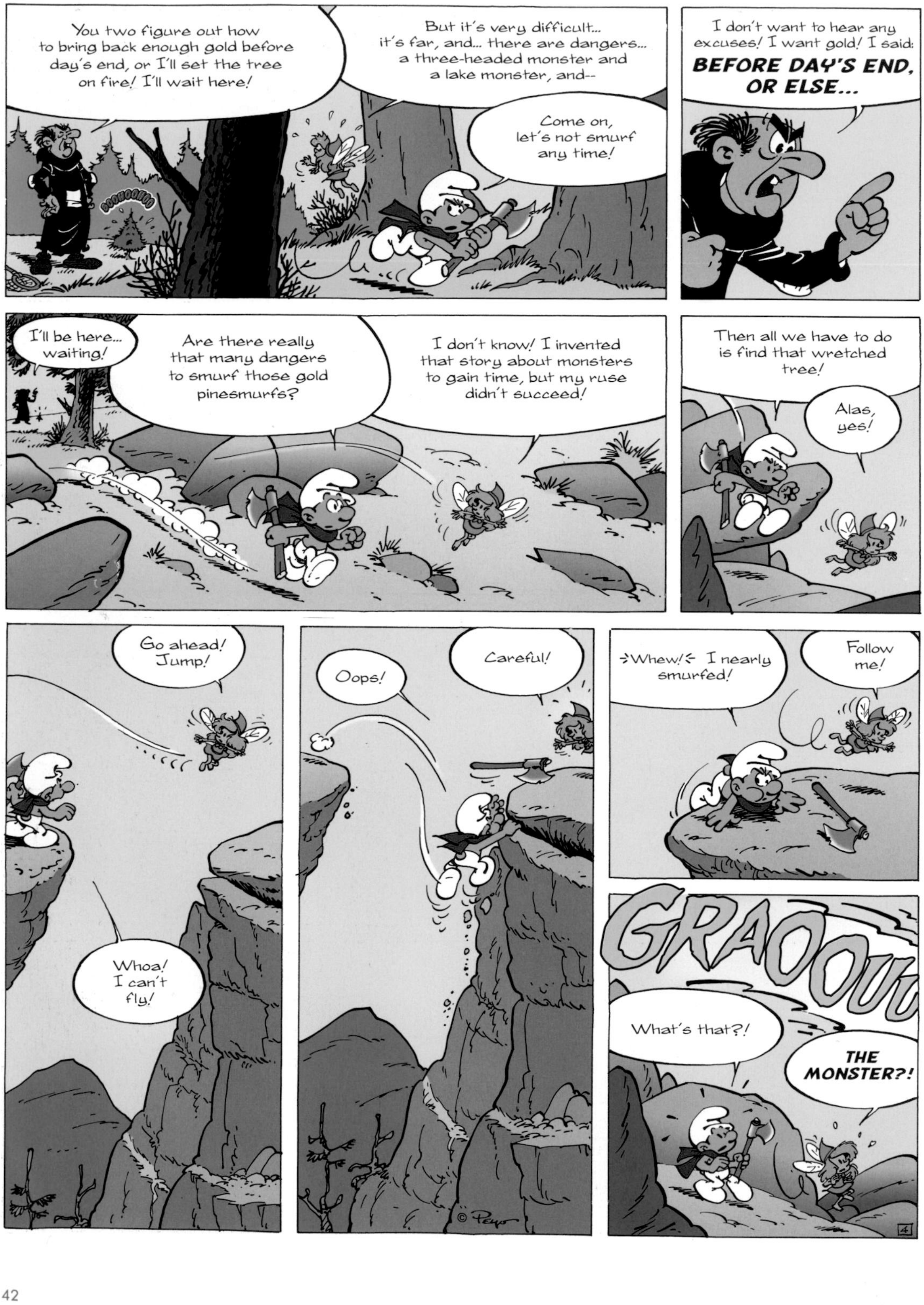
You two figure out how to bring back enough gold before day's end, or I'll set the tree on fire! I'll wait here!
But it's very difficult... it's far, and... there are dangers... a three-headed monster and a lake monster, and--
Come on, let's not smurf any time!
I don't want to hear any excuses! I want gold! I said: BEFORE DAY'S END, OR ELSE...
I'll be here... waiting!
Are there really that many dangers to smurf those gold pinesmurfs?
I don't know! I invented that story about monsters to gain time, but my ruse didn't succeed!
Then all we have to do is find that wretched tree!
Alas, yes!
Go ahead! Jump!
Whoa! I can't fly!
Oops!
Careful!
Whew! I nearly smurfed!
Follow me!
GRAOOUU
What's that?!
THE MONSTER?!
© Peyo
4

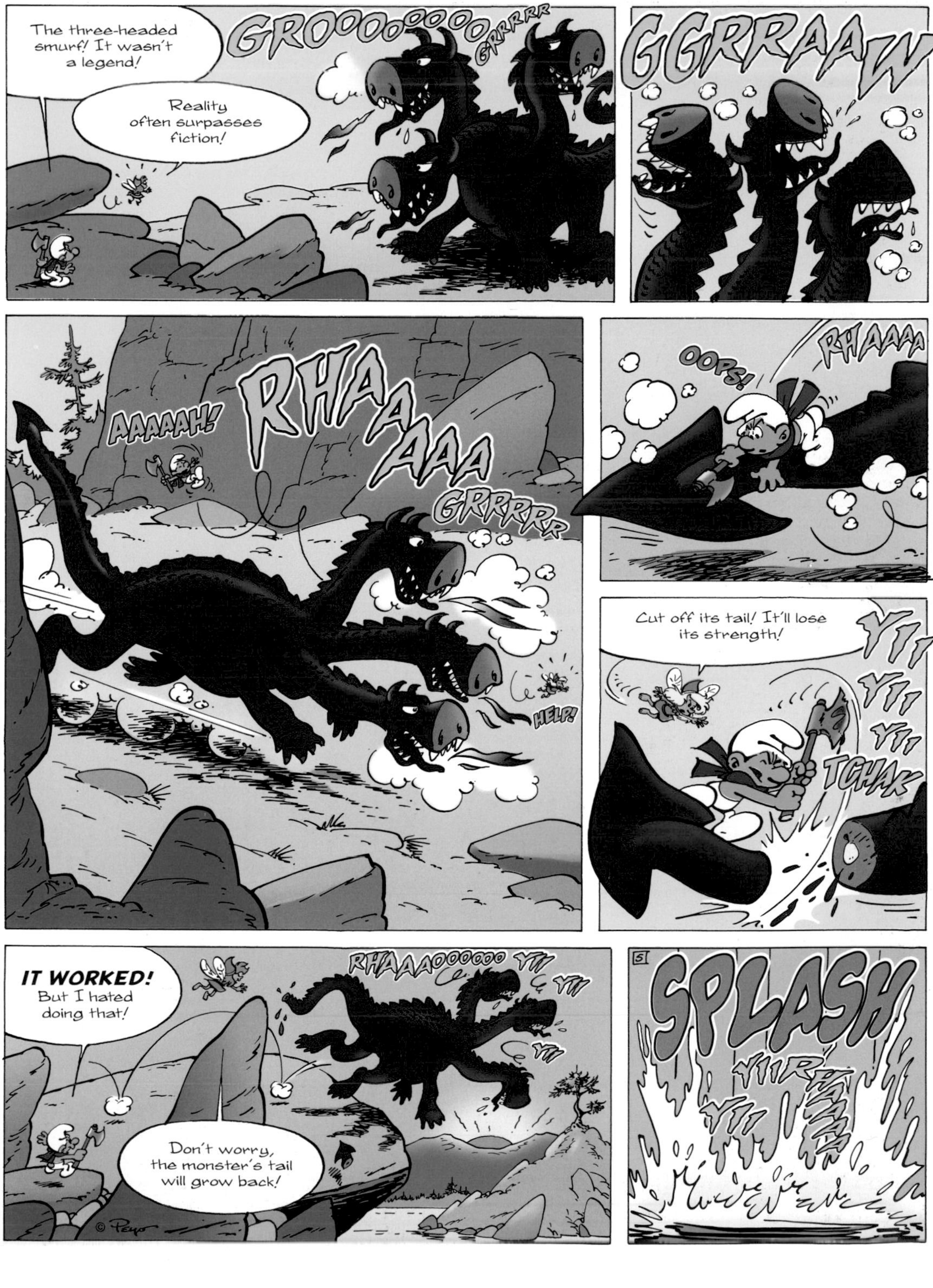
The three-headed smurf! It wasn't a legend!
GROOOoOOOOO GRRRRR
Reality often surpasses fiction!
GGRRAAW
AAAAAH!
RHAAAAA
GRRRRRR
HELP!
OOPS!
RHAAAA
Cut off its tail! It'll lose its strength!
YII YII YII
TCHAK
IT WORKED! But I hated doing that!
RHAAAOOOOOO YII YII
YII
Don't worry, the monster's tail will grow back!
© Peyo
5
SPLASH
YIIR
YII

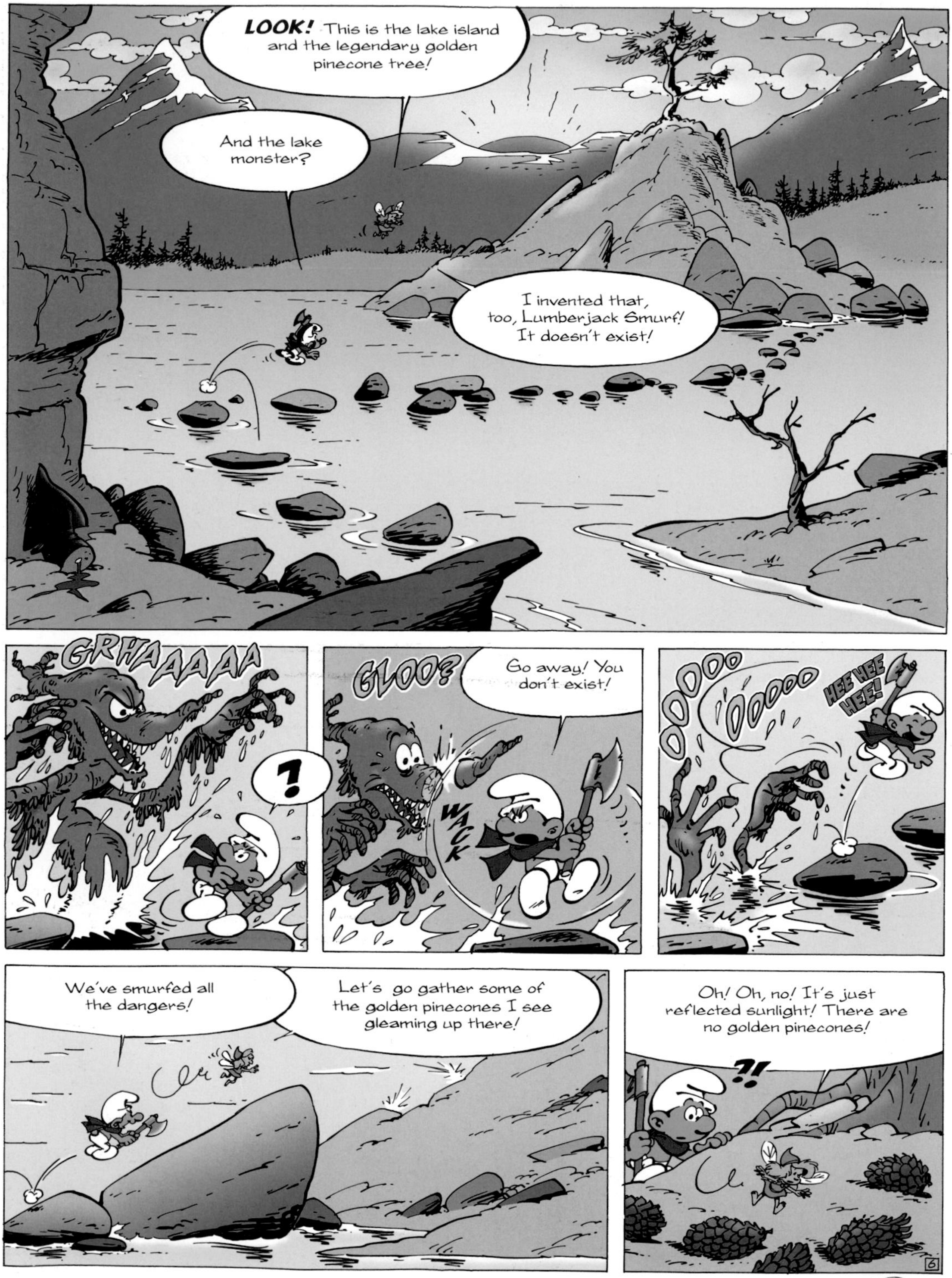

LOOK! This is the lake island and the legendary golden pinecone tree!
And the lake monster?
I invented that, too, Lumberjack Smurf! It doesn't exist!
GRHAAAAAA
?
GLOO?
Go away! You don't exist!
WACK
OOOOO OOOOO
HEE HEE HEE!
We've smurfed all the dangers!
Let's go gather some of the golden pinecones I see gleaming up there!
Oh! Oh, no! It's just reflected sunlight! There are no golden pinecones!
?!!
6

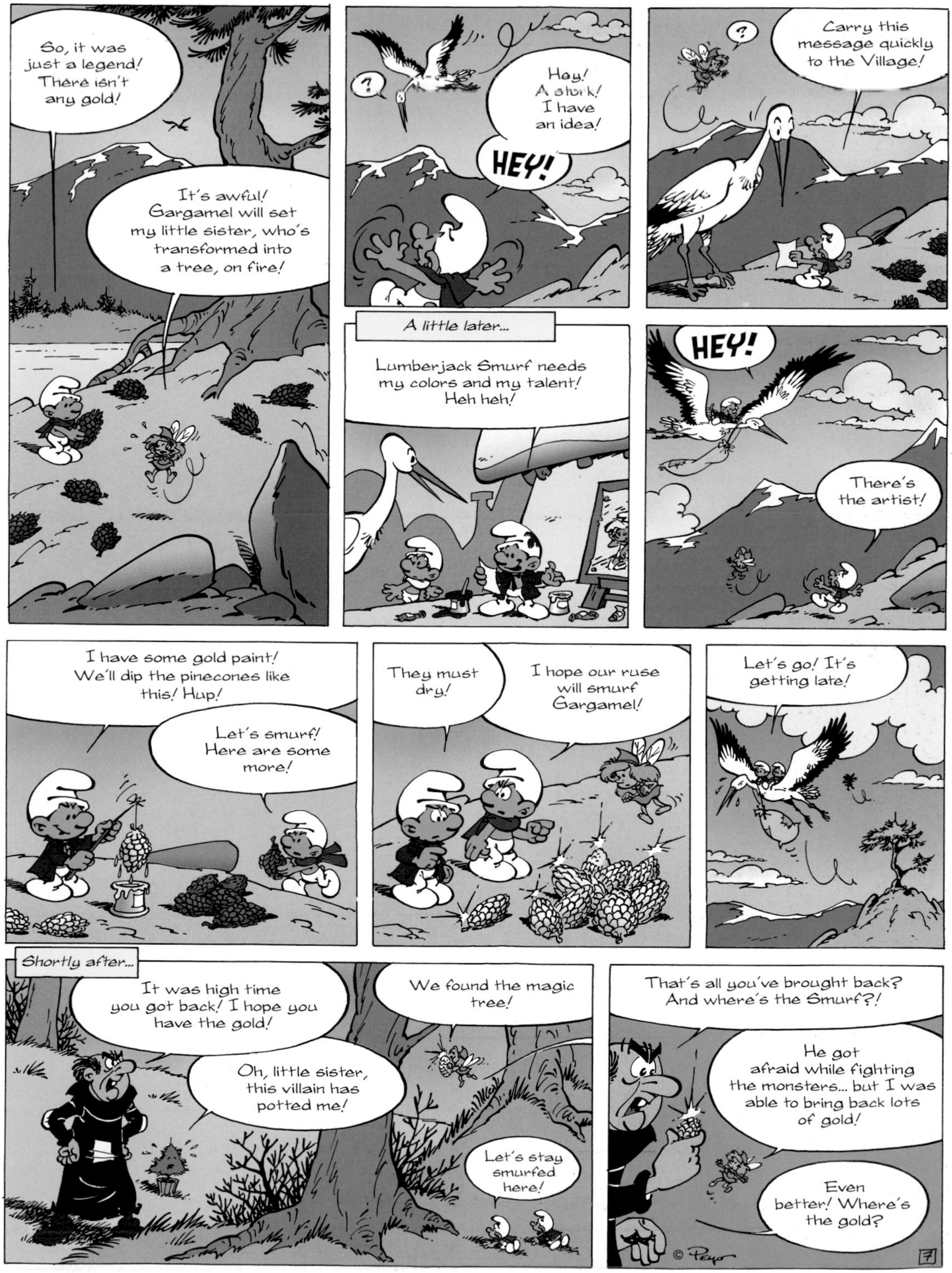

So, it was just a legend! There isn't any gold!
It's awful! Gargamel will set my little sister, who's transformed into a tree, on fire!
Hey! A stork! I have an idea!
HEY!
Carry this message quickly to the Village!
A little later...
Lumberjack Smurf needs my colors and my talent! Heh heh!
HEY!
There's the artist!
I have some gold paint! We'll dip the pinecones like this! Hup!
Let's smurf! Here are some more!
They must dry!
I hope our ruse will smurf Gargamel!
Let's go! It's getting late!
Shortly after...
It was high time you got back! I hope you have the gold!
Oh, little sister, this villain has potted me!
We found the magic tree!
Let's stay smurfed here!
That's all you've brought back? And where's the Smurf?!
He got afraid while fighting the monsters... but I was able to bring back lots of gold!
Even better! Where's the gold?
© Peyo
7

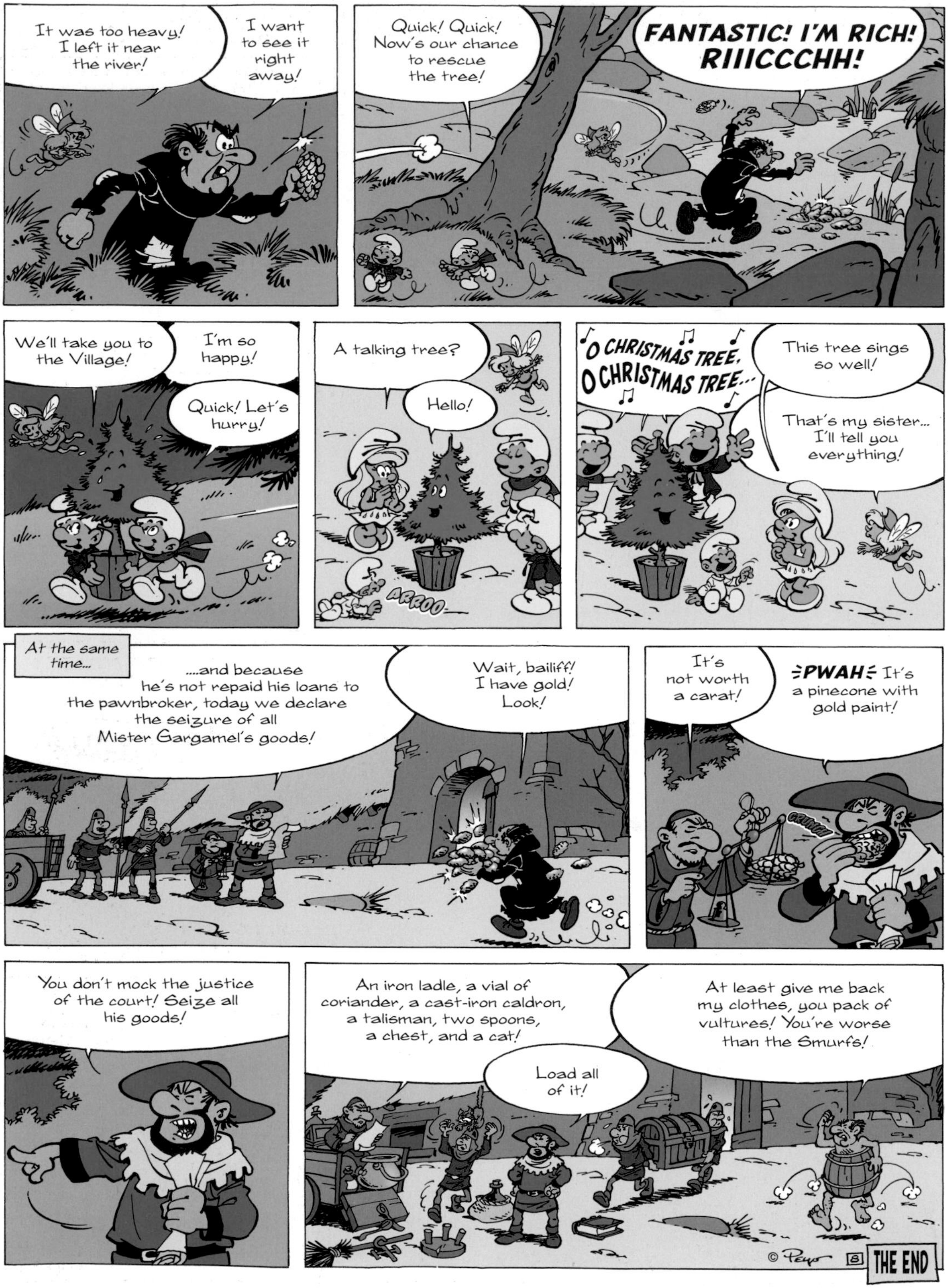
It was too heavy! I left it near the river!
I want to see it right away!
Quick! Quick! Now's our chance to rescue the tree!
FANTASTIC! I'M RICH! RIIICCCHH!
We'll take you to the Village!
I'm so happy!
Quick! Let's hurry!
A talking tree?
Hello!
ARROO
O CHRISTMAS TREE, O CHRISTMAS TREE...
This tree sings so well!
That's my sister... I'll tell you everything!
At the same time...
...and because he's not repaid his loans to the pawnbroker, today we declare the seizure of all Mister Gargamel's goods!
Wait, bailiff! I have gold! Look!
It's not worth a carat!
PWAH It's a pinecone with gold paint!
You don't mock the justice of the court! Seize all his goods!
An iron ladle, a vial of coriander, a cast-iron caldron, a talisman, two spoons, a chest, and a cat!
Load all of it!
At least give me back my clothes, you pack of vultures! You're worse than the Smurfs!
© Peyo
8
THE END

THE SMURFS CHRISTMAS

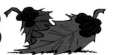

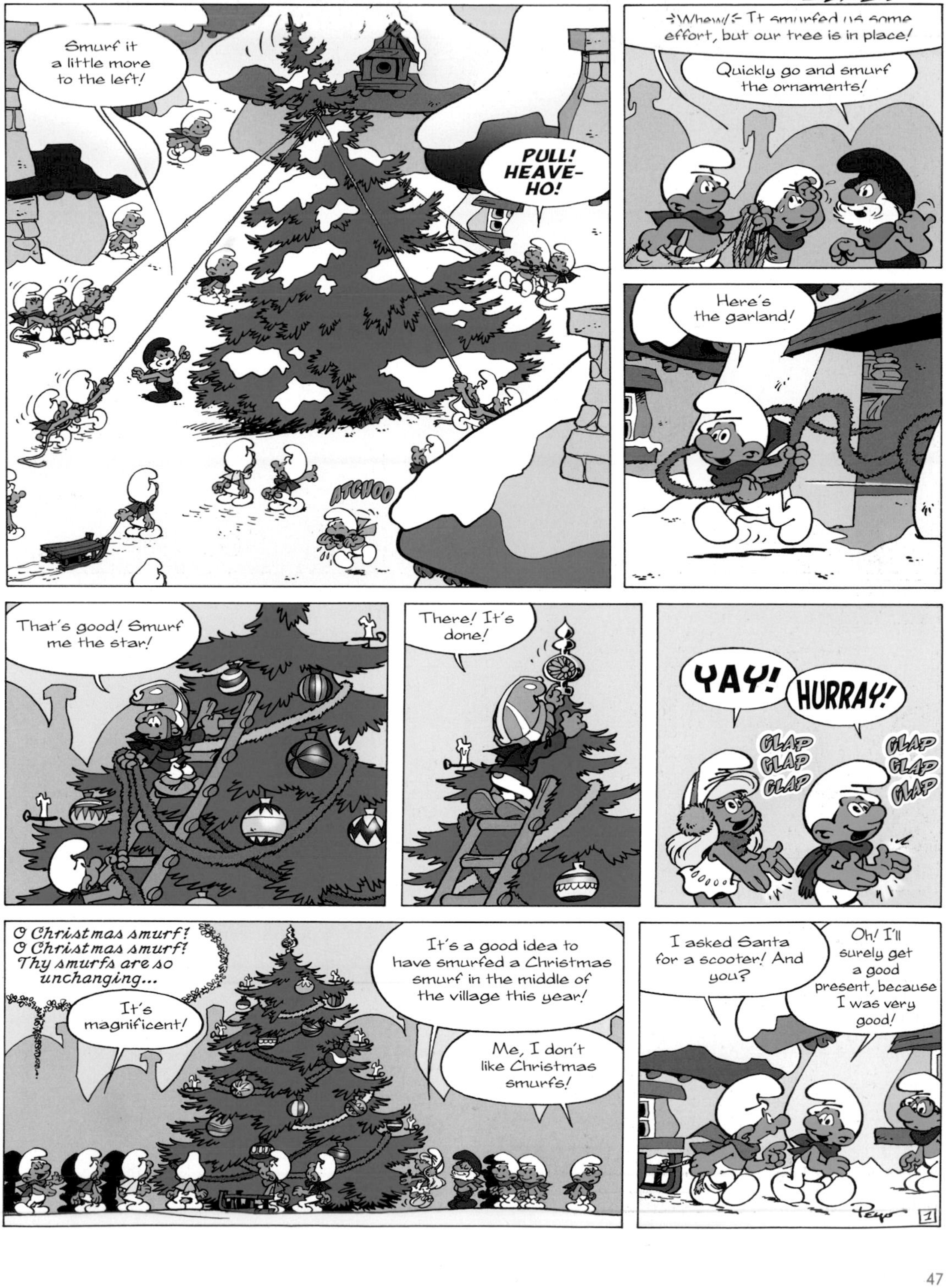
Smurf it a little more to the left!
PULL! HEAVE-HO!
ATCHOO
Whew! It smurfed us some effort, but our tree is in place!
Quickly go and smurf the ornaments!
Here's the garland!
That's good! Smurf me the star!
There! It's done!
YAY!
HURRAY!
CLAP CLAP CLAP
CLAP CLAP CLAP
O Christmas smurf! O Christmas smurf! Thy smurfs are so unchanging...
It's magnificent!
It's a good idea to have smurfed a Christmas smurf in the middle of the village this year!
Me, I don't like Christmas smurfs!
I asked Santa for a scooter! And you?
Oh! I'll surely get a good present, because I was very good!
Peyo
1

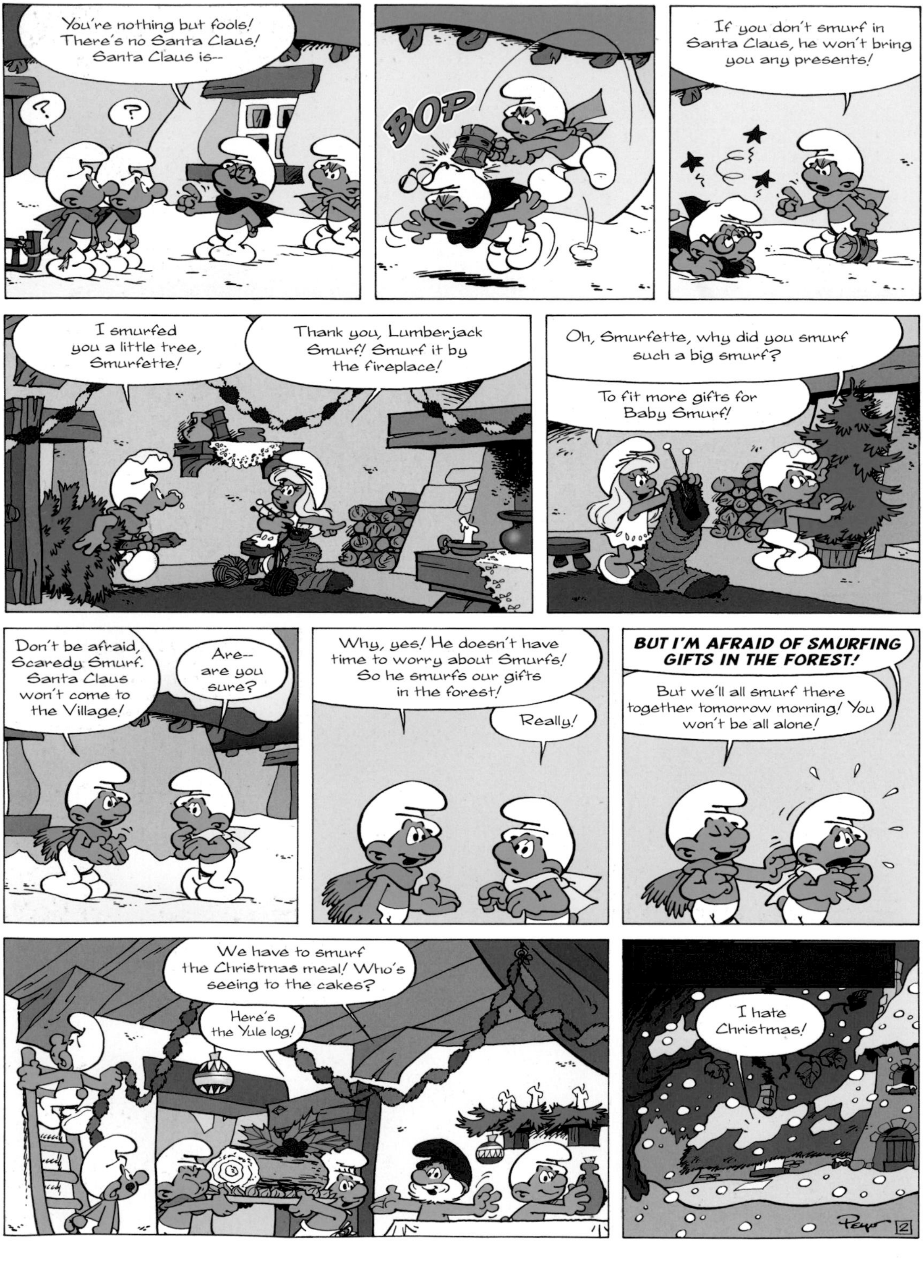
You're nothing but fools! There's no Santa Claus! Santa Claus is--
?
?
BOP
If you don't smurf in Santa Claus, he won't bring you any presents!
I smurfed you a little tree, Smurfette!
Thank you, Lumberjack Smurf! Smurf it by the fireplace!
Oh, Smurfette, why did you smurf such a big smurf?
To fit more gifts for Baby Smurf!
Don't be afraid, Scaredy Smurf. Santa Claus won't come to the Village!
Are-- are you sure?
Why, yes! He doesn't have time to worry about Smurfs! So he smurfs our gifts in the forest!
Really!
BUT I'M AFRAID OF SMURFING GIFTS IN THE FOREST!
But we'll all smurf there together tomorrow morning! You won't be all alone!
We have to smurf the Christmas meal! Who's seeing to the cakes?
Here's the Yule log!
[redacted]
I hate Christmas!

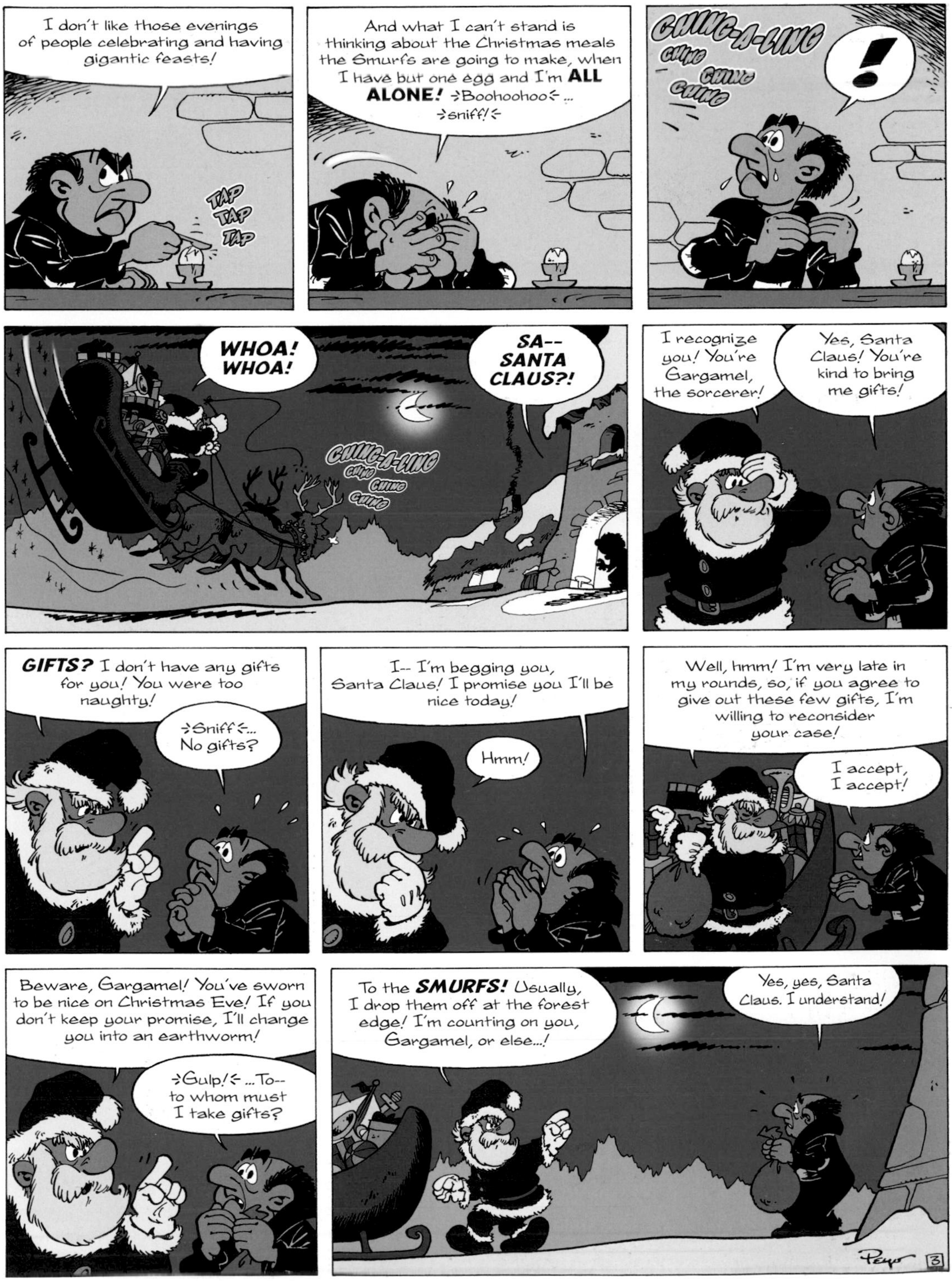

I don't like those evenings of people celebrating and having gigantic feasts!
TAP TAP TAP
And what I can't stand is thinking about the Christmas meals the Smurfs are going to make, when I have but one egg and I'm **ALL ALONE!** >Boohoohoo< ... >sniff!<
CHING-A-LING CHING CHING CHING
!
WHOA! WHOA!
SA-- SANTA CLAUS?!
CHING-A-LING CHING CHING CHING
I recognize you! You're Gargamel, the sorcerer!
Yes, Santa Claus! You're kind to bring me gifts!
GIFTS? I don't have any gifts for you! You were too naughty!
>Sniff<... No gifts?
I-- I'm begging you, Santa Claus! I promise you I'll be nice today!
Hmm!
Well, hmm! I'm very late in my rounds, so, if you agree to give out these few gifts, I'm willing to reconsider your case!
I accept, I accept!
Beware, Gargamel! You've sworn to be nice on Christmas Eve! If you don't keep your promise, I'll change you into an earthworm!
>Gulp!< ...To-- to whom must I take gifts?
To the **SMURFS!** Usually, I drop them off at the forest edge! I'm counting on you, Gargamel, or else...!
Yes, yes, Santa Claus. I understand!
Peyo
3

Don't forget your promise, Gargamel, if you don't want to end your days in an earthworm's skin!... Ho, ho, ho, ho, ho....!

CHING-O-LING CHING CHING CHING

Me, Gargamel, giving Christmas gifts to the Smurfs! ⸗RHAAAA!⸗ What a horrible fate!

Oh, but, thinking about it...! I could take advantage of this to lay some traps and capture those cursed Smurfs! Heh heh heh heh heh...!

Don't forget your promise, or else I'll change you into an earthworm!

⸗GULP!⸗

I have no other choice! If I don't keep my promise, Santa Claus will know and punish me!

Meanwhile in the Village...

Hurry up, Grouchy Smurf, the party's getting started! We'll all have fun together!

Me, I don't like having fun all together!

On this Christmas Eve, to all the Smurfs, I'd like to say...

Peace on smurf to all Smurfs of good will and **MERRY CHRISTMAS!**

MERRY CHRISTMAS!

♪ SANTA CLAUS IS SMURFING TO TOWN, HE'S... ♪♪

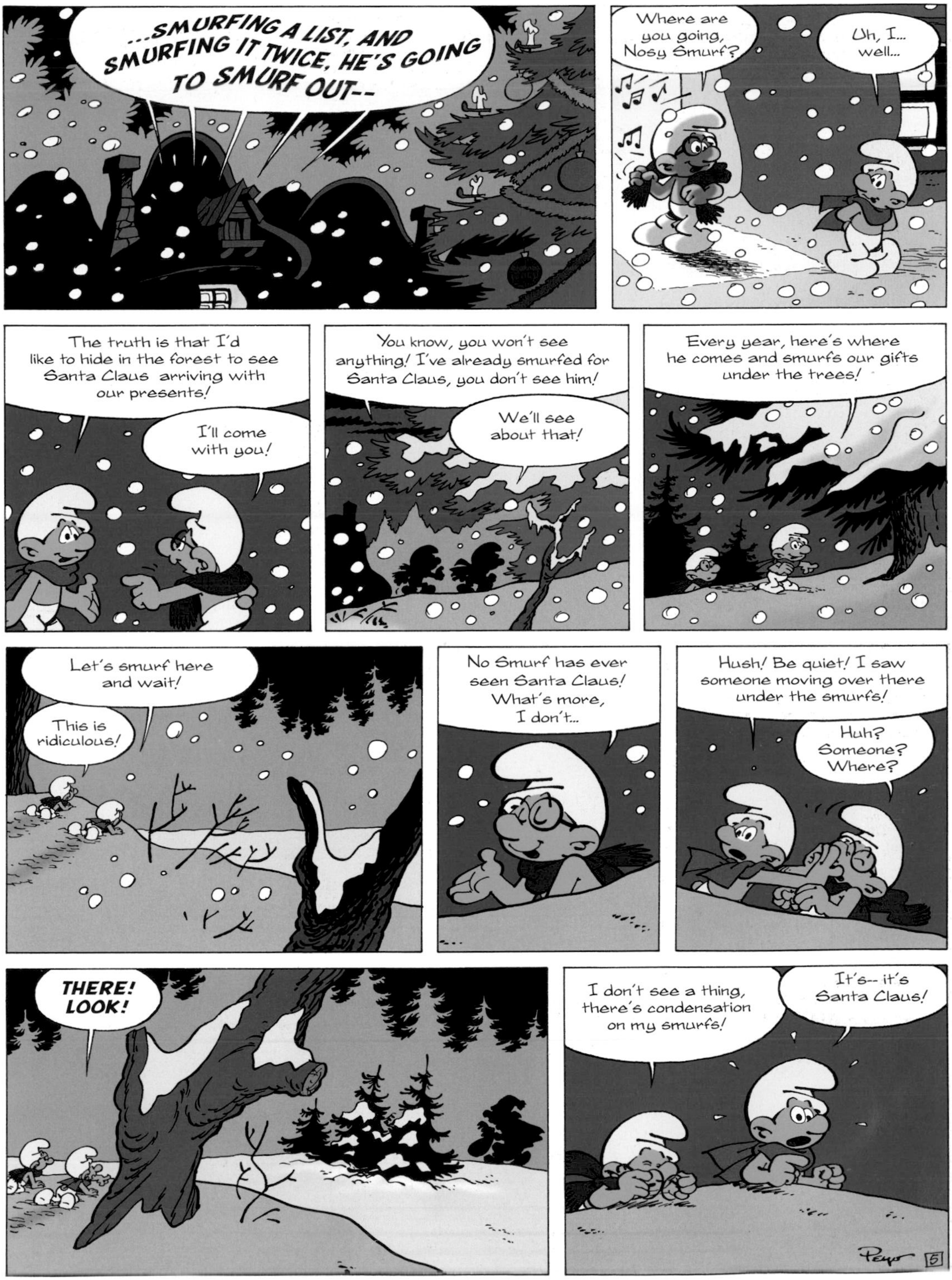
...SMURFING A LIST, AND SMURFING IT TWICE, HE'S GOING TO SMURF OUT--
Where are you going, Nosy Smurf?
Uh, I... well...
The truth is that I'd like to hide in the forest to see Santa Claus arriving with our presents!
I'll come with you!
You know, you won't see anything! I've already smurfed for Santa Claus, you don't see him!
We'll see about that!
Every year, here's where he comes and smurfs our gifts under the trees!
Let's smurf here and wait!
This is ridiculous!
No Smurf has ever seen Santa Claus! What's more, I don't...
Hush! Be quiet! I saw someone moving over there under the smurfs!
Huh? Someone? Where?
THERE! LOOK!
I don't see a thing, there's condensation on my smurfs!
It's-- it's Santa Claus!
Peyo
5

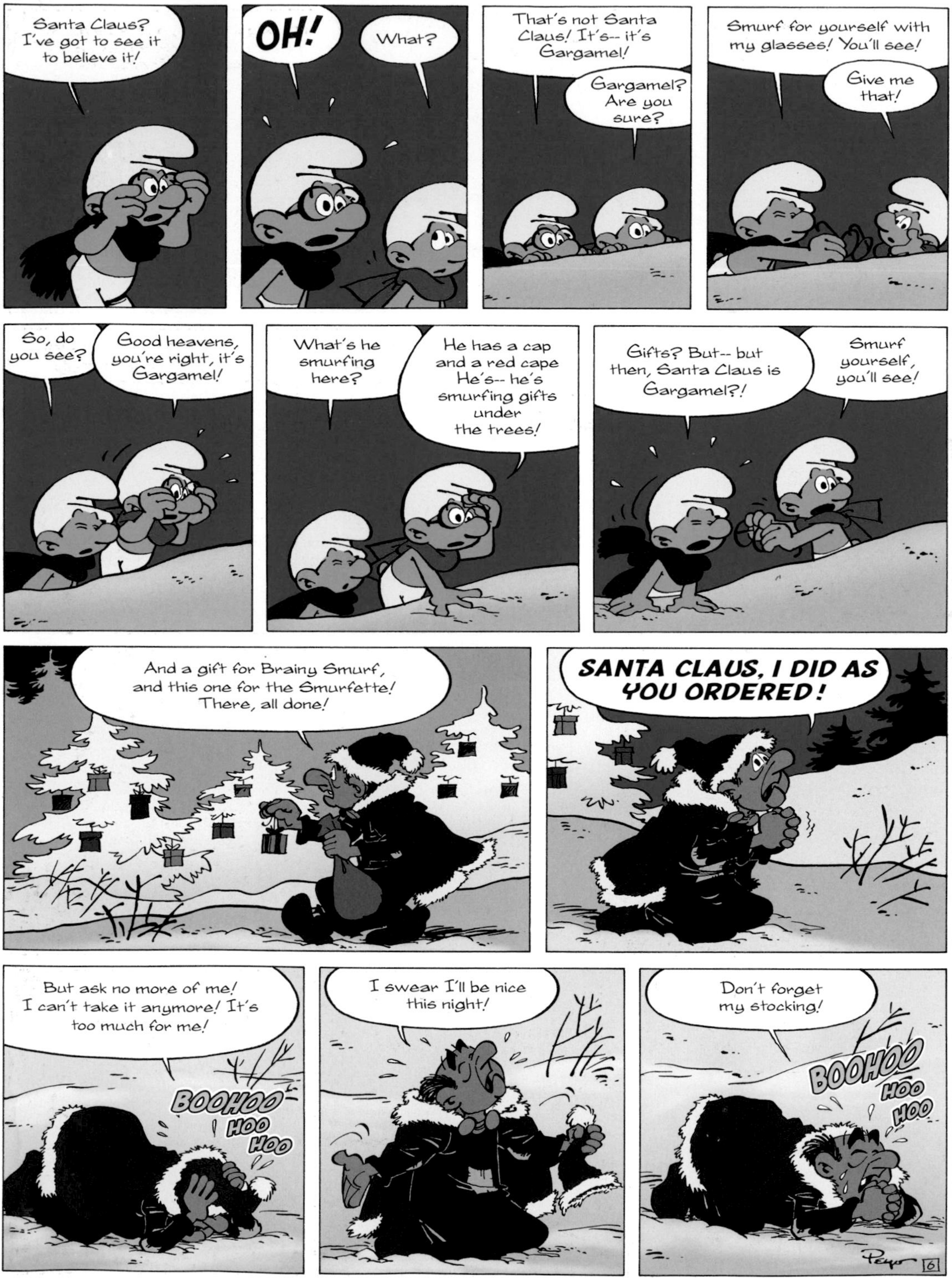
Santa Claus? I've got to see it to believe it!
OH!
What?
That's not Santa Claus! It's-- it's Gargamel!
Gargamel? Are you sure?
Smurf for yourself with my glasses! You'll see!
Give me that!
So, do you see?
Good heavens, you're right, it's Gargamel!
What's he smurfing here?
He has a cap and a red cape He's-- he's smurfing gifts under the trees!
Gifts? But-- but then, Santa Claus is Gargamel?!
Smurf yourself, you'll see!
And a gift for Brainy Smurf, and this one for the Smurfette! There, all done!
SANTA CLAUS, I DID AS YOU ORDERED!
But ask no more of me! I can't take it anymore! It's too much for me!
BOOHOO HOO HOO
I swear I'll be nice this night!
Don't forget my stocking!
BOOHOO HOO HOO
Peyo
6

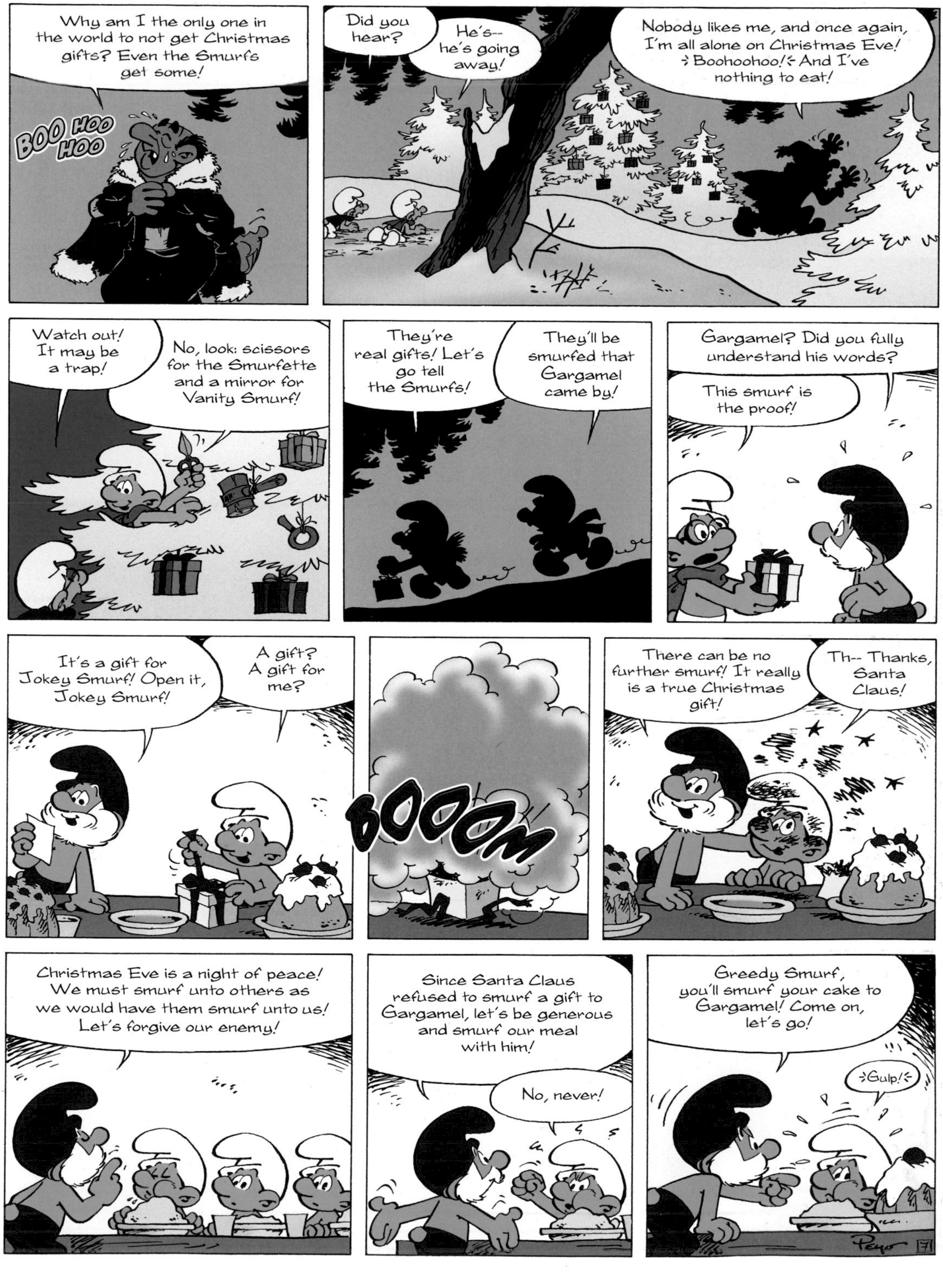

Why am I the only one in the world to not get Christmas gifts? Even the Smurfs get some!
BOO HOO HOO
Did you hear?
He's-- he's going away!
Nobody likes me, and once again, I'm all alone on Christmas Eve! Boohoohoo! And I've nothing to eat!
Watch out! It may be a trap!
No, look: scissors for the Smurfette and a mirror for Vanity Smurf!
They're real gifts! Let's go tell the Smurfs!
They'll be smurfed that Gargamel came by!
Gargamel? Did you fully understand his words?
This smurf is the proof!
It's a gift for Jokey Smurf! Open it, Jokey Smurf!
A gift? A gift for me?
BOOOM
There can be no further smurf! It really is a true Christmas gift!
Th-- Thanks, Santa Claus!
Christmas Eve is a night of peace! We must smurf unto others as we would have them smurf unto us! Let's forgive our enemy!
Since Santa Claus refused to smurf a gift to Gargamel, let's be generous and smurf our meal with him!
No, never!
Greedy Smurf, you'll smurf your cake to Gargamel! Come on, let's go!
Gulp!
Peyo 71

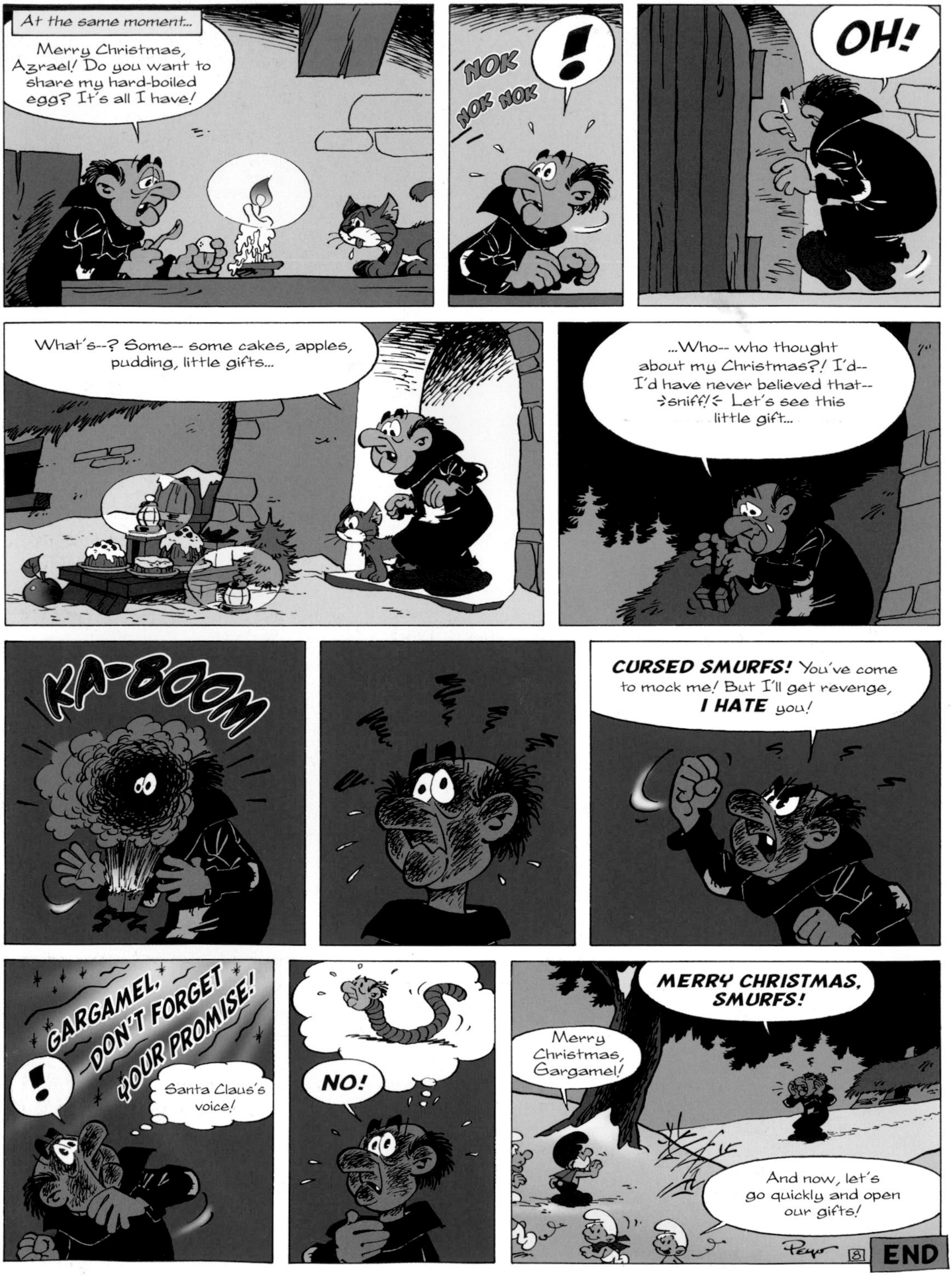
At the same moment...
Merry Christmas, Azrael! Do you want to share my hard-boiled egg? It's all I have!
NOK NOK NOK
!
OH!
What's--? Some-- some cakes, apples, pudding, little gifts...
...Who-- who thought about my Christmas?! I'd-- I'd have never believed that-- →sniff!← Let's see this little gift...
KA-BOOM
CURSED SMURFS! You've come to mock me! But I'll get revenge, I HATE you!
GARGAMEL, DON'T FORGET YOUR PROMISE!
!
Santa Claus's voice!
NO!
MERRY CHRISTMAS, SMURFS!
Merry Christmas, Gargamel!
And now, let's go quickly and open our gifts!
Peyo
8
END

WATCH OUT FOR PAPERCUTZ™

Monster Christmas
PAPERCUTZ

GARFIELD
HOME FOR THE HOLIDAYS
PAPERCUTZ

GARFIELD
CAROLING CAPERS
PAPERCUTZ

CLASSICS Illustrated Deluxe
Scrooge
PAPERCUTZ

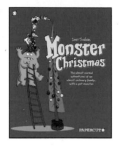

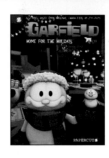

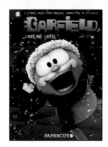

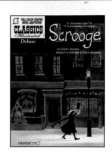

Welcome to THE SMURFS CHRISTMAS graphic novel from Papercutz, the place where happy little elves are dedicated to publishing great graphic novels for all ages. I'm Jim Salicrup, the Smurf-in-Chief, wishing you a Happy Holiday Season!

Whether you celebrate Christmas or not, there are certainly some wonderful values expressed in these stories that are worth remembering year-round — such as caring for those less fortunate and being kind to everyone, even your so-called "enemies."

For even more holiday comics fun, may I suggest MONSTER CHRISTMAS by the world-famous cartoonist, Lewis Trondheim? It's the almost-normal adventures of an almost ordinary family... with a pet monster. For Christmas, the family goes on vacation to the mountains. Kriss, their pet monster, is supposed to stay at home, but he manages to make the trip on the roof of the car. Suddenly an avalanche blocks the road, caused by another monster in hot pursuit of... Santa Claus! It's up to the kids and Kriss to Save Santa and Christmas!

Then there's CLASSICS ILLUSTRATED DELUXE #9, which presents "A Christmas Carol" together with another Charles Dickens treasure, "Mugby Junction," a lesser-known tale, that we're sure you'll love. Estelle Meyrand's expressionist artwork brings a rich palette and dynamism to these two classic Christmas tales by one of the World's Greatest Authors.

Finally, there are two holiday-themed volumes of GARFIELD & Co — #4 "Caroling Capers," in which Garfield decides to sing carols in hope of getting rewarded with holiday foods, and #7 "Home for the Holidays," a touching tale that features Garfield's struggle to find the true spirit of Christmas.

Not only would these graphic novels make a great addition to your home library, they make great presents for friends and family! And unlike Jokey Smurf's presents, these won't blow up in your face!

We hope you enjoy these and many other Papercutz graphic novels, not only during the holiday season, but all year round. There's a certain kind of joy found only in comics (or to use the fancy-schmancy term "graphic novels") that you can enjoy anywhere and anytime. And who can't use a little more joy in their lives?

Happy Holidays, Blue-Buddies!

Jim

STAY IN TOUCH!

EMAIL: Salicrup@papercutz.com
WEB: www.papercutz.com
TWITTER: @papercutzgn
FACEBOOK: PAPERCUTZGRAPHICNOVELS
SNAIL MAIL: Papercutz, 160 Broadway, Suite 700, East Wing, New York, NY 10038

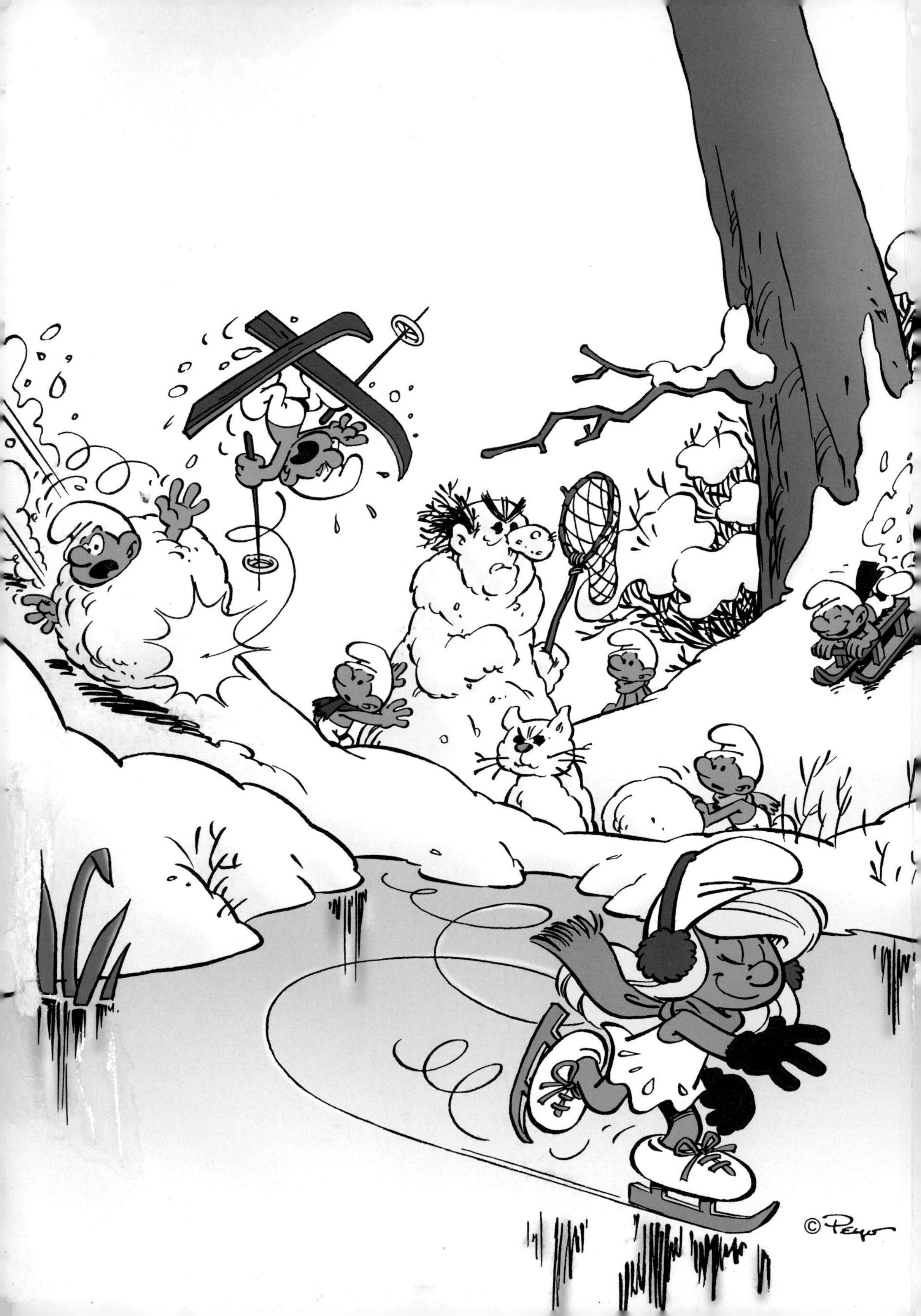
© Peyo